paiN
sluts

Also available from STORGY Books:

Exit Earth
Shallow Creek
Hopeful Monsters
You Are Not Alone
This Ragged, Wastrel Thing
Annihilation Radiation
Parade

STORGY®
BOOKS

STORGY® BOOKS Ltd.
London, United Kingdom, 2021

First Published in Great Britain in 2021 by STORGY® Books

London

Grateful acknowledgement is made to the following publications in which some of these stories were first published: Scribble Magazine, 'God and the Runt'; STORGY Magazine, 'Shaving for Dog', 'Death and the Teenage Stripper', 'Consumed' (first published as 'Can You Eat the Wind?'); STORGY Books, 'Trevor's Lost Glasses'; The Fiction Pool, 'Werewolf'.

Published by STORGY® BOOKS Ltd.
London, United Kingdom, 2021

10 9 8 7 6 5 4 3 2 1

Cover Design by Dean Cavanagh & Tomek Dzido

Edited & Typeset by Tomek Dzido

A CIP catalogue record for this title is available from the British Library

Trade Paperback ISBN 978-1-9163258-4-5
eBook ISBN 978-1-9163258-5-2

www.storgy.com

pain sluts

Sian Hughes

To Philip,
for always believing.

CONTENTS

Tell all the truth but tell it Slant -

— Emily Dickinson

Sometimes it feels like we are only this: moments of knowing and unknowing one another. A sound that is foreign until it's familiar. A drill that's a scream until it's a drill. Sometimes it's nothing more than piecing together the ways in which our hearts have all broken over the same moments, but in different places. But that's romantic. Sometimes it's realer than that.

— T Kira Madden
Long Live the Tribe of Fatherless Girls

And I wonder about
this lifetime with myself,
this dream I'm living.
I could eat the sky
like an apple
but I'd rather
ask the first star:
why am I here?
why do I live in this house?
who's responsible?
eh?

— Anne Sexton
The Fury of Sunsets

CONSUMED

'You haven't lost the pregnancy. But I can't find a heartbeat.'

The sonographer's sentences don't belong together. Scanning her face for more clues, Amy notices that she has a tan face and white neck, like parts from different bodies.

'Can I see?' she says.

The sonographer points at the screen. In a corner of Amy's womb, floating with its back to her, in sulky suspended animation, is a shape.

'There's the blood flow from the placenta,' the sonographer says, as a tide of grainy darkness flows in from the edge. 'But there's no fetal heartbeat.'

The sonographer continues to circle the image, shaking her head. It occurs to Amy that it could all be a problem of technology: a mouse that doesn't work, a frozen cursor. But when a nurse standing next to the cubicle's curtains leaves suddenly, Amy knows it isn't that. And yet she is still confused. The baby is gone but not gone. It is an anomaly Amy can't process, like seeing the light from a dead star.

'I'll get the doctor,' says the sonographer.

On Saturday evening Amy bleeds. A pink-gray embryo sac falls onto the stained gusset of her knickers.

She shouts for Rob three times.

'You need to calm down,' says Rob, walking into the bathroom finally. 'Connie'll freak out.'

Even though Amy loves her stepdaughter: Connie with the jagged shoulder blades that stick out like wings; Connie who says spaghetti with 'daleks' instead of spaghetti with garlic; a sudden hatred for her husband works itself through Amy's body like a contraction. Through the skin of the embryo sac, the blurry outline of something emerges.

'I'll get towels,' says Rob, looking away.

Amy doesn't know what to do with the embryo sac. Flushing it down the toilet as if it's a goldfish or shit is unthinkable. Interring it in the freezer seems worse. Wrapping it in a parcel of quilted toilet paper, Amy stuffs it in her dressing gown pocket.

'I don't know what to do with it,' she says to Rob, as they're watching a Netflix thriller later.

Amy has begun to picture the baby drying inside the toilet paper like snot: the paper sticking to the surface of the sac.

'Bury it,' says Rob, and then, out of the blue, as cops drag a dead girl out of a lake, 'Can't help thinking you're enjoying this.'

'Fuck you,' she says, storming to the kitchen.

In the kitchen, Amy studies the spice jars on the rack. Emptying the contents of the fenugreek jar into the compost caddy, she fills it with oil. There is a tremor, a kind of convulsion, as she drops the sac into the oil. The sac spreads and expands in the fluid. Amy sees the beginnings of legs, a spine curling inwards like a comma, a single eye meeting hers.

'Hi little one,' she says.

'Sorry about last night,' says Rob, the following morning. 'Guess I freaked out.'

Amy clasps her fingers around the jar inside her dressing gown as if it were a secret.

'I'm fine Rob,' she says.

'I'll try to be back by lunch,' he says. 'We could go out?'

Amy pushes the jar deeper into the pocket of her gown, careful not to push it through a tear in the seam that was once a slit but is now a gaping hole.

'Maybe,' she says, pulling the belt of her dressing gown tighter. 'If you're back.'

After Rob has left, Amy relocates the spice jar to the drawer of her nightstand. Every hour, on the hour, she climbs upstairs, as if she were visiting somebody in hospital. By eleven the egg sac is unravelling: silky fibres unwrap themselves from around the baby's torso, giving the impression of somebody undressing.

Amy covers the jar in a tea towel.

At midday, Amy collects Connie from nursery, takes her to the park around the corner. Connie plays in the bushes behind the perimeter railings, pretending to be a zookeeper looking for a lost lion. A strong wind blows in from the west.

'Can you eat the wind?' says Connie, running over to Amy's bench.

Amy normally likes the weird things Connie says. But today Amy is desperate to return to the other child. She has remembered a story about a friend of her great auntie Edie's, Beattie Bevan, who kept a baby in ethyl alcohol on her dresser.

'Let's go home shall we?' says Amy. 'It's getting cold.'

Settling Connie in front of the television, Amy checks in on the baby. Apart from a few shreds of egg sac, stuck to his forehead like transfers, the baby is naked. Waxy strips float to the surface of the oil.

Amy googles 'how to preserve a foetus'. Her search returns a Daily Mail story about a mother who kept a foetus in an ice cube tray in a freezer, You Tube videos about preserving chicken embryos in acrylic.

At two, Rob calls to say he's stuck at work.

'Wasn't expecting you anyway,' says Amy.

'Oh, ok' he replies. 'How's the bleeding?'

It's the first time Rob has asked about the bleeding. Amy knows she should be grateful. But Amy doesn't give a fuck about the bleeding. She only gives a fuck about the baby. If anything, she likes the way the bleeding has left her feeling light-headed and insubstantial. The fact Rob knows so little about her dredges up the bitterness she so often feels.

'I got blood on the Ercol,' she says. 'It won't come off.'

The Ercol chair is Rob's prize possession. Amy is pleased that she bled on it.

'Fucksakes,' he says.

When Rob gets home, Amy makes her excuses and retires early to bed. Having repositioned the jar under her pillow for safekeeping, she tries to sleep. The edge of the jar presses through the pillow into her cheek, carving out nightmares. When she wakes, it is to the idea that someone has stolen the baby. She yanks the jar from under the pillow.

The egg sac has completely disintegrated; remains hang down from the surface in an assortment of gray and white tatters like bunting. Amy resists the urge to shake the jar like a snow globe to bring it back to life. At the same time, the baby is as beautiful as ever. Following the contours of its body, Amy sees the head bent over onto the chest as if in prayer; tiny mounds where there would have been ears; the suggestion of toes.

'Rob!' she calls.

Rob is asleep in the guest bedroom, one leg poking out of the duvet.

'Rob!' she says again. 'I need to show you.'

Putting the jar on the nightstand beside him, Amy turns on the lamp. The baby glows orange between them. Amy counts the stitches under Rob's left nipple as she waits for him to respond. There are meant to be nine stitches, but she can only count seven.

'You need to see a therapist Amy,' he says, finally. 'It's not normal.'

A wave of loneliness hits her with such force she almost loses her balance. She grabs the jar from the nightstand.

'We lost another baby, and you couldn't give a fuck.'

Afterwards, Amy sits on the toilet lid in the bathroom, waiting for the morning, for normality, for something. She imagines sitting on the toilet lid for hours and days and months, watching her face age in tiny increments in the mirror. At the same time, she wants things to return to normal. To start over. It troubles her that she can't remember the number of stitches on her husband's body.

Taking the jar from the pocket of her dressing gown, which feels heavier now, weighted, Amy stares at the baby, who has his back turned. Suddenly she wants the baby back inside her, where it belongs. She wants him alive again, like he was in the sonographer's office, to exist in space, if not in time, like stone babies fossilized inside their mother's abdomens.

Tipping it out of the jar into her palm and lifting it to her face, Amy strokes the tiny body, a final caress from crown to rump, before swallowing her baby whole.

WEREWOLF

Today's lovers are even closer to Angela's house than usual, their Kia Picanto squeezed into a triangle of tarmac where Lovers Layby tails off.

Angela puts the cleaning cloth on the windowsill, as a bilious, clawing sensation rises in her. The heat generated by the lovers seems to have passed through her skin to the core of her. She screws down the cap on the Windolene.

'This can't go on, Pete!' she yells. 'It's disgusting.'

Pete is watching tele in the conservatory, wearing his noise cancelling headphones, which silence ninety percent of ambient noise. Last week, over dinner, he claimed they made him feel like an astronaut in outer space.

'Oh forget it!' says Angela.

Angela knocks on Val's old house at number one. In her hand is the petition she's written.

As she waits for her new neighbour, Mira, to appear, Angela's attention shifts to a midi-skip spewing out carpets on the drive: rolls of Axminster that were once Val's pride and joy

'C'mon Ange, we were all young once!' Mira says, when Angela shows her the petition calling on the Council to install CCTV on the cemetery gates overlooking Lovers Layby. 'They're not doing any harm.'

Angela doesn't like Mira. She doesn't like being called Ange, which sounds like a nasty germ-laden sneeze. She doesn't like the fact Mira and her partner Mike (a hedge fund manager with an accent Angela can't place), are slowly erasing her memories of Val, so much so that Angela finds herself questioning whether Val even lived at number one, or whether she always lived in The Burrows nursing home, in a room so small they put her wardrobe in the bathroom.

'I wrote it myself. Took me all night,' she says. 'Val would have felt the same.'

'I'm sorry,' Mira says.

Martin at number three is more understanding.

'It's not just couples, Angela,' he says. 'Last week I saw a man masturbate. He was in a green Ford Sierra.'

Martin's lips have an ashy bluish tinge that suggests he has a heart condition. Angela wonders whether Martin's increasingly crude language is symptomatic of his illness.

'Legally, masturbating in broad daylight is an act of gross indecency,' he whispers. 'I saw him ejaculate.'

The explosive 'j' and 't' consonants in 'ejaculate' send flecks of dense creamy spittle into Angela's décolletage.

'So will you sign the petition?' says Angela, stepping back.

'I don't like CCTV,' says Martin. 'But if you need to talk, I'm always here.'

'Martin thinks it could be against the law—all those shenanigans in the layby,' Angela says to Pete when she gets home. 'Gross indecency,' he said.

'Then ask Martin to deal with it,' he says. 'He likes doing you *favours*.'

Last time Pete was away on business, Martin had wheeled their bins up the drive. Angela was on the phone to Talk Talk at the time, arguing over a mid-contract price hike, when she felt a tap on her shoulder.

'I put the bins out, but the pin's gone.'

Martin was behind her on the welcome mat, holding up the broken lid of their wheelie bin like a trophy.

'Long screw's what you need Angela,' he said. 'Then bob's your uncle.'

Maggots wriggled on the hinge of the bin lid. A shift in air density made it harder to breathe.

'A long screw and a bottle cap works a treat.'

'I'm on the phone Martin,' she'd said. 'I'll deal with it later. Thank you.'

Martin drew his hand away, his thumb grazing Angela's bosom by mistake. A maggot tumbled downwards like confetti. Later, when Angela told Pete about the incident, she added details. Martin skimmed her nipple *and* breast, she said. Her nipple was erect from the draught.

'Huh. Say what you like about Martin. Least he doesn't spend all day wallowing about in his La-Z-Boy watching rubbish on TV,' she says.

'Too busy being a peeping Tom,' says Pete, reaching for his neck brace, which Angela knows he only wears to avoid intimacy.

'Carry on like that and you won't be able to hold yourself up!' says Angela. 'Physio insists you don't need it.'

'Physio's even more of a prick than Martin,' says Pete.

Angela takes the layby petition with her to The Burrows for her weekly visit to Val.

When she gets there, the nursing home is hosting a party to celebrate the completion of the sun patio. There are jam sandwiches, chocolate fingers, French fancies. Shafts of sunlight pour in through the new bi-fold doors, lighting up Val's cheek.

'It's like Sodom and Gomorrah in the layby now,' says Angela, handing Val the petition. 'You wouldn't believe what they get up to. Ych a fi.'

'It's a re-le-vation,' says Val, squinting at the petition. 'I can see so much better without my glasses. You have to work harder but at least everything isn't jumping out at you.'

'Mira won't sign it,' says Angela. 'Too busy tearing your carpets out.'

Val finishes the doughnut that's been balancing on the arm of her chair. Another resident lifts one half of a turtleneck jumper, revealing a breast shaped like a scythe.

'Nobody wants to see your boobies Betty!' says a care worker, running over.

'They're being over-stimulated!' says Angela. 'Too much sugar.'

Val shakes her head in disagreement, causing custard to zigzag through her chin hairs.

Angela swabs at Val's face with a wet wipe.

'Bloody hated those carpets anyway,' says Val, flinging the petition to the floor. 'All the swirls gave me migraines. I used to think about ramming the house down with the fucking car.'

Before coming to The Burrows, Val never used the word fuck. The word fuck distresses Angela. She pictures Val ramming the door of number one with her Allegro; the bonnet crashing into Mira's new Corian kitchen island.

'I'll bring it back next week,' says Angela, peeling the petition from the floor. 'There'll be fewer distractions.'

Angela kisses Val goodbye on the cheek. Val's thickly applied face powder leaves a residue like animal down on Angela's lips.

'You used to be a werewolf,' says Val, inexplicably.

'Get some rest please Val,' says Angela.

Pete has made chicken dinner by the time Angela arrives home.

'I been thinking,' he says, plating up. 'There was a notice on the community board about a book club. First Tuesday every month. You could do with an outlet.'

'I've gone off books,' says Angela.

Angela likes books, but not as much as she used to. She is angry with Pete for always assuming he knows what she needs, when the truth is, he hasn't a clue.

'Books don't do it for me.'

Angela scrapes chicken leftovers into the recycling caddy under the sink, her ass pointing at Pete like a gun.

'Val told me I used to be a werewolf,' she says. 'I think she's got dementia. Or a tumour.'

'A werewolf?' says Pete.

Angela imagines Pete hoisting up her skirt, parting her ass cheeks. When she stands up to straighten her skirt, a pea lands on the tiles between her feet. Angela crushes the pea into the grouting until it's dead. Why should she pick it up, or talk, or do anything, when Pete doesn't even notice when her ass is as engorged as those pink mandrill asses on nature programmes?

'Is there something wrong?' says Pete.

'I'm fine thank you Peter,' says Angela.

Angela wanders around the house doing nothing. Pottering around, dilly dallying, going to waste. She sorts through the clothes that need donating, throwing them back in the wardrobe in a heap. She reads the blurb and a few pages of her thriller. At some point it occurs to her she might be coming down with something: a chill, a foreign virus, the C word.

As she's passing the staircase window on her way to bed, a black Audi pulls into Lovers Layby. The driver eases his seat back, sending a creaky shiver through Angela's solar plexus.

'We should never try to deny the beast—the animal within us,' says a voice.

Pete is in the hallway by the console table, wearing a werewolf mask.

'The Howling, 1981,' he says. 'Classic.'

'What the hell are you playing at?' says Angela. 'You trying to kill me?'

Pete takes a step towards Angela, tugging off an all-over latex mask with protruding muzzle, matted faux hair, yellow fangs with fake tartar and blood.

'Don't you remember? Derek gave it to us. When he shut down the fancy-dress stall. You wore it to that Halloween party in Caldicot. Val came. And Alan. That's what she was on about today.'

Pete throws the mask into the under-stairs cupboard.

'Thought wearing it would jog your memory,' he says, demoralised.

'God knows what you're talking about,' says Angela. 'You're as senile as Val.'

That night, Angela dreams she is trapped in a layby: a sweeping semi-circle of tarmac that has no function because the carriageway is already wide enough. She and Peter are in their old car. The Cavalier. Pete is on top of her, dead. In her panic, she knocks off the hand brake. The car lurches like a ghost car towards the carriageway.

Going downstairs, she finds Pete lying on his stomach on the wicker sofa in the conservatory, arms wrapped around a queer-smelling cushion.

'I'm coming now,' he says, half-asleep.

'You were snoring again,' she says. 'I could hear you through the ceiling like a dog.'

'That's impossible. I've been awake this whole time.'

Angela pictures severing Pete's dangling uvula with nail scissors to stop him snoring. Suffocating him with the orthopaedic memory foam pillow from JML. Leaving him. Lying beside him, huffing loudly, she tugs a throw across the scrag ends of her knees.

'I thought you should know,' she says. 'I remember the party.'

'Oh,' he says. 'Ok.'

After the layby dream, there'd been a second dream; though it wasn't a dream but a memory. She and Pete were on their way back from the Halloween party in Caldicot. They'd stopped at a service station in a rest area for lorries. Pete used the sheet of his ghost costume to cover the stick between the seats. It was the best sex she'd ever had.

'It was fun,' she says. 'We used to have fun Pete.'

'We were young. I'm sixty-one.'

'I know. It's not really your fault.'

The werewolf mask is resting on top of Pete's toolbox in the under-stairs cupboard when Angela retrieves it in the morning.

Sniffing at the guard hairs and lining, Angela tugs the mask over her head. Through the eye-holes the hall is unfamiliar, as though she's trespassing through somebody's house.

Back upstairs she uses a clothes brush to smooth the hair down, spraying tingly clouds of cherry-scented dry shampoo into the pale grey under-fur, removing the dust with a wet wipe. Without thinking, she begins to peel off her clothes.

When she's naked, except for the mask, she checks her reflection in the mirrored wardrobe doors, adjusting their angles until she appears as a series of infinite indestructible reflections, stretching backwards and forwards in space.

The white-grey werewolf fur falls into the dipped curves of her collarbone, framing her breasts, contrasting with the glossy dark bird's nest of her pubes. Lifting her forearm to the muzzle, she tastes the luscious long-forgotten saltiness of her flesh.

Afterwards she visits Val at the nursing home.

'Hope to Christ you haven't brought that Ryvita muck again,' says Val.

Val has a condition called late-onset Type 1 diabetes. As a rule, Angela brings a selection of healthy snacks to the nursing home: crackers, easy-peel oranges, sugar-free jelly pots, water. But today she has brought other things. A multipack of Twix, two blue Monster drinks, a dragon fruit that was on sale in the reduced aisle.

Val sucks the Twix like it's a drug.

'I want to die happy. Slip into a diabetic coma,' she says. 'I can't go back.'

'Don't know what came over me,' says Angela.

Angela pulls the mask from her carrier bag.

'Here's that werewolf you were talking about,' she says, placing it next to the Twix pack and dragon fruit on Val's over-chair tray table. 'It was a Hallowe'en party we went to in Caldicot. You and Alan came. That's the mask I wore.'

Val strokes the fur on the muzzle, her lips lined theatrically with chocolate.

'You had a tail hanging from your pussy like a cock,' she says.

Earlier, whilst wearing the werewolf mask, Angela had masturbated in the guest room, as rays of late afternoon sunshine swished across her ass, her naked haunch. In the mask, she felt more like herself.

'What was I?' says Val, quite suddenly. 'I can't remember.'

Val holds the mask to her face, inhaling deeply.

Angela takes the mask from Val's hand. Val clamps her hand to Angela's wrist.

'Who was I at the party?' she says. 'Who was I?

In the evening, when a Honda Civic pulls into Lovers Layby, Angela reaches for Pete's woollen greatcoat from the banister, which still smells of Aramis from years back.

'I'm going for a walk,' she shouts. 'Won't be long.'

Light filters through the blinds in Martin's study as Angela passes number three. A grinning Martin peers through a fissure in his blinds, his shirtless torso glowing eerily. Fondling the rough hairs of the werewolf mask she secreted earlier in Pete's pocket, Angela follows the curve of the pavement around the cul-de-sac's turning circle, until she's on the same side of the road as the layby.

The Honda is parked at a skewed angle to the pavement as though abandoned. Keeping to the shadow of the wall, Angela pulls on the werewolf mask. Walking purposefully towards the car, as her skin fuses to the latex of the mask, she creeps on bended knees along the Honda's nearside.

At first, she sees nothing except limbs. A low-resolution assortment of parts splayed unnaturally across the front seats. She knocks on the passenger window. But the music, a house remix of something she once knew, renders the knocking inaudible, and for a moment she wonders how loud the music would need to be to crack all the windows in the cul-de-sac, to penetrate Pete's foam cocoon.

She knocks a second time, then a third, rapping hard on the glass with her wedding ring. The woman in the passenger seat turns her head in slow motion, owl-like. Imperfectly blended lines of shimmering cream highlighter map the outer edges of her cheekbones, the ridge of her nose; streaks of gold fizz like comets through her hair. Angela can barely bear it: this beauty.

'You shouldn't be here. It's not fair,' she says, through the muzzle.

The woman's mouth becomes a dark oval hole.

'Go!' shouts Angela, as the car careens down the cul-de-sac towards the carriageway. 'Don't come back!'

Angela stuffs the mask back in her pocket. She feels guilty but high all the same. It wasn't so much that she wanted to scare off the lovers or punish them. She simply needed to reclaim the cul-de-sac.

As she retraces her steps around the turning circle, a cat leaps from Martin's end wall, yowling on contact with the road. Angela phones Val from her mobile.

'You were the woman in Cat People,' she says. 'I just remembered. Sorry if I woke you but …'

'I'm still awake,' says Val. 'I'm never awake beyond nine. It's the blue drink I think.'

'You had a velour black catsuit,' says Angela.

'I had silk fucking whiskers out to here,' says Val, after a pause. 'My tail was even longer than yours.'

'You should get to sleep now,' says Angela.

'We'll speak tomorrow,' says Val.

When Angela arrives home, Pete is waiting for her by the console table in the hallway, in the neck brace and noise-cancelling headphones.

'Where were you? I looked everywhere,' he says.

'I have to do everything myself,' she says. 'You never listen.'

'They're streaming the Day of the Dead trilogy in HD,' he says. 'I'm recording it.'

Angela walks past her husband towards the conservatory, fishing out the remote control from the side of the La-Z-Boy, switching the tele off.

'Take off the brace' she says. 'We need to fuck.'

BRONTOSAURUS

Margaret is at the foot of her daughter Cerys's hospital bed holding an eighteen-inch helium balloon.

'Hunted high and low for it,' she says.

'It's pretty,' replies Cerys. 'Really pretty.'

The balloon obscures half Margaret's face: the bulge of its coral pink surface echoing an eruption of rosacea on Margaret's cheek. Printed on the surface of the balloon, in lemon-sherbet lettering, are the words 'It's a GIRL!'

'Tescos, Wilkinsons, Aldis, you name it! Pipsqueak in Asda couldn't speak English properly. Said they didn't sell them 'no more'!'

'Sounds like a nightmare mum. You didn't need to.'

Cerys's husband Jim rises from his seat beside the bed with a sigh and says he's off to get coffee from the machine. Margaret winds a length of curly balloon string around the baby's bassinet, pausing briefly to peer inside. Having kicked off her cellular blanket, the baby is gazing blankly into nowhere.

'Want to hold her?' asks Cerys. 'She's been fed.'

'Uh huh. Once I've fixed this balloon,' says Margaret.

The balloon bobs above the bassinet like a moon, drifting higher and higher as the string fights itself free. Margaret double-knots the string to the bassinet, yanking at the frame, causing the whole thing to skid away from the bed.

'Damn thing!' says Margaret. 'What's wrong with a normal cot?'

The baby's cry is like a fault in the earth cracking open. Cerys lifts her up from the bassinet.

'Shh Grug,' she says. 'Mammy's here for you.'

It isn't until after Cerys has been discharged from hospital the following afternoon that she remembers about the balloon.

'Shit. It's still on the bassinet,' she says to Jim, as he pulls up outside their house.

Margaret's navy Volkswagen saloon is parked on the pavement up ahead, sporting a new oversized 'Grandchild On Board' bumper sticker. The plan is that she's staying in their spare room until the weekend.

'She's bound to notice.'

'It's a balloon, babes,' says Jim, squeezing the steering wheel. 'Corporate plastic shit. Can't believe they're not banned already.'

Jim is a development officer at a conservation charity. He and Cerys met at a wild swimming fundraising event on the Gower peninsula.

'It's ok for you,' says Cerys. 'Your parents don't give a toss.'

Tricia, Jim's mother, is an electrosensitive who runs a yoga retreat in a wireless dead zone in County Mayo. His father lives somewhere in north Wales.

'They're not control freaks, if that's what you mean,' says Jim.

Margaret is staring out at them from the lounge window as they exit the car. From the subtle slant of her body, Cerys immediately spots signs of a problem.

'Been worried sick,' says Margaret, as they enter the house. 'Nasty crash on the Ynysforgan roundabout. Thought you might phone to let me know you're ok.'

'No news is good news, Margaret,' replies Jim.

Groundwater from the crawl space beneath the floorboards has evaporated to leave a musty smell in the hallway. Cerys flicks on the electric air freshener and lights.

'I'll go help Jim, mum,' says Cerys, handing her mother the baby. 'You cwtch with Grug.'

'Three fatalities,' whispers Margaret. 'I was worried sick.'

Cerys retrieves her baby changing bag from the backseat of the car as a gust of wind sweeps over the exposed small of her back. Jim removes holdalls from the boot.

'That it then?' says Margaret, looking over Cerys's shoulder towards the car, once they're back inside the house. 'Is that *all* of it?'

Cerys thinks back to the ward. As she and Jim signed various discharge forms, the balloon cleaved to a pale slice of light on the wall behind the bassinet, quietly leaking air through a tiny hole in its neck. Cerys could have transferred it to the handle of the infant carrier then and there, but the truth was something stopped her. After that she'd forgotten all about it.

'Think so,' she says. 'Yes.'

Margaret turns her face to the wall, tracing the rosacea with her finger.

'So, I'll make us tea shall I?' says Cerys.

'I'll make my own thank you,' says Margaret.

That night Cerys can't sleep. Waking to a sense of foreboding, a sensation so strong it makes her queasy, she reaches into the basket to check on Grug. As she does so, she hears footsteps on the landing.

Rushing back to bed, pulling the duvet up to her ears, Cerys knows from the long pauses between footsteps that her mother is heading for their bedroom. Jim is asleep with his back to her, his skin a queer orangey-white colour like the atmosphere of a distant planet.

'I didn't want to embarrass you last night in front of Jim, what with it being your first day home,' whispers Margaret from the doorway. 'But, well, where's that balloon I bought you?'

A tide of yellow lamplight from the landing sweeps across the floorboards as Margaret opens the door a little further. Cerys pretends to be asleep, lightly shifting her body beneath the duvet to make her movements resemble those of a sleeping person. But the duvet is a dead body on top of her: an immense crushing weight.

'I walked all the way to that new Morrisons you know, Cerys. No pavement or lighting under the bridge. Could have been mugged or stabbed or God knows what. Your great auntie Cathy was lying in the hallway for three days before anyone found her.'

'It's in the car, mum,' Cerys says, finally, emerging from beneath the duvet to breathe. 'I'll get it in the morning, ok?'

Streetlights flicker on outside the bedroom window.

'Good. I was worried,' says Margaret.

Pale watery sunshine casts the street in a reassuring everyday light as Cerys makes her way to the car in the morning, and for a split second she forgets that she's a grown woman pretending to look for a non-existent helium balloon in the back of an empty Skoda Yeti. But when pretence and procrastination is no longer possible, Cerys glances back to the house. Her mother is back by the now open window: same position, same problem.

'I'll check underneath the car, mum. The string might have caught on the wheel,' she shouts.

Cerys sinks to her knees to inspect the car's undercarriage, where she finds herself in the same position as she assumed for childbirth: down on all fours, her slits visible, a bleating animal.

'What are you doing?' a familiar voice asks.

Looking up, she sees Jim standing on the kerb, holding Grug.

'It's the balloon,' she whispers. 'I'm pretending to look for it.'

Grug is making a curious chewing motion with her lips: hunger.

'Do you want me to tell her? This is nuts.'

Cerys checks the window, but her mother is now nowhere to be seen.

'No,' says Cerys. 'I should do it.'

Cerys carries Grug into the lounge, fully expecting her mother to barge in on them and continue questioning her about the balloon. Resting the baby's head in the crook of her arm, she tries to remember the lactation consultant's instructions:

Tummy to tummy.

Nose to nipple.

Skin to skin.

But the angle of the baby's head is all wrong. The light in the room is all wrong. Everything is wrong. Instead of focusing on

Grug, Cerys finds herself rehearsing what to say to her mother. *I'm sorry. It was chaos. You know what it's like. It's only a balloon. I'll buy another one.* Aiming her nipple upwards so that the darkly pigmented disc of her aureole is in line with the baby's bottom lip, she tries again to make the baby latch on. But the baby, weary from crying, slides off the scarped edge of her nipple.

'You left it there deliberately.'

Cerys quickly yanks a muslin cloth over her breast, but her mother, wearing a mint-green pants suit, fuchsia lipstick, heavy concealer, has already colonised the armchair in the alcove. Cerys wonders if she's been there all along? Watching. Studying her daughter's leaky ineffectual cow tits.

'You're being ridiculous mum,' says Cerys. 'It's only a balloon.'

There, she said it. It wasn't difficult. With decisive effort, the muslin cloth thankfully concealing most of her left breast, Cerys squishes her nipple between thumb and forefinger and feels a release of pressure as Grug finally latches on.

'I'll buy another one ok?' she says, to soften the blow.

But Margaret is running her middle finger through a fine layer of dust on the dado rail. Back in the summer, when a pelt of allergens coated every surface in their old Victorian house, Margaret had developed a sudden dust mite allergy. Her eyes watered. Her nose ran. A lunar tinge suffused her skin. Cerys already knows that her failure to expunge the dust from the dado rail is, as far as Margaret is concerned, evidence of the same casual treachery that led her to forgetting the balloon.

'We could go back to the hospital this afternoon if you prefer. Once it's stopped raining,' Cerys adds, unconvincingly. 'It'll still be there.'

A flat afternoon light filters through the north-facing lounge window, giving Margaret's body such a solid outline that it renders the rest of the room artificial, irrelevant, remote. Rising from the armchair, Margaret approaches the sofa and gently kisses Grug on the still-soft part of her skull, as if for the final time.

'You left if there because you hate me, Cerys,' she says.

A familiar gut-wrenching guilt rises through Cerys's body like subsurface water. She considers chasing after her mother down the hallway, but Grug is still sucking on her nipple, her ear lobes wriggling with pleasure.

'Mammy's not going anywhere, baby,' she whispers. 'I promise.'

Cerys tells herself that everything will be okay. Her mother will eventually come around: adjust to the reality of being a grandmother (or whatever else was bugging her). With feeding-time finally finished, she positions Grug on the sofa beside her, inside a palisade of brightly coloured scatter cushions, securing the horseshoe-shaped breastfeeding pillow around her baby's head. But no sooner has Cerys closed her eyes to rest for a while than Jim is at the foot of the sofa.

'She's gone,' he says. 'I looked everywhere.'

'She's right here,' says Cerys, confused, assuming he's referring to Grug.

'Your mother. Cleared out the bedroom. Packed all her fucking stuff. I've tried ringing.'

'She was here a minute ago,' says Cerys.

'You've been asleep.'

Drawing the flap of her breastfeeding cardigan across her body, Cerys focuses on the belt loops for longer than necessary. A blackbird lands on the hydrangea outside the window and shimmies around on a thin branch before flying off out of view.

'She thinks I forgot the balloon because I hate her.'

Margaret's Volkswagen is still parked outside the house as they set off in search of her, having left another two messages on voice mail.

'She won't have gone far,' says Cerys, gesturing at her mother's car.

'Slammed the front door so hard she could have broken the bloody glass,' says Jim. 'Fucking asshole.'

'Your parents haven't even called. I don't know what's worse,' says Cerys

They drive to the gardening centre with the overpriced coffee shop, and then to the mini-market, and then to the park with the war memorial and bandstand. When they fail to find her in any of the usual haunts, Cerys directs them into the cul-de-sac that leads to the municipal cemetery behind their street.

'She likes that creepy old tomb at the top,' she says.

A group of teenage girls gathered at the bus stop stares at them as they drive their car towards the cemetery gates. Cerys opens the window.

'You seen a woman in a pants suit? Mint green? About seventy years old. Grumpy looking?'

Jim slams his foot on the gas and sends them flying over a speed bump.

'What's wrong with asking people?' she says.

'It's a farce,' he says, pulling up in the cemetery parking area. 'She's a Grade A fucking narcissist.'

Cerys watches her husband mope along the tree-lined footpath that leads to the remembrance garden. At some indistinct point he becomes opaque: his shadow merging with even larger shadows cast by towering cypress trees. Suddenly it seems absurd to Cerys that a man she has only known for two years is now her husband and the father of her child. The chance of meeting your soulmate was around one in ten thousand, she'd read, so this man was almost certainly an imposter. But if he was, then so was she.

'You should take Grug home,' says Jim, when he returns to the car, ten minutes later. 'I'll keep looking.'

'It's ok. I'll stay.'

'Look. It's bad enough that I have to go look for fucking Mommie Dearest, without worrying about you and the baby. So please Cerys. Just go. I won't be long.'

It's almost dark by the time Cerys arrives home. Margaret's car remains parked outside their house.

'We normally tell people to wait 24 hours,' says the call handler, when Cerys dials 101.

Cerys goes over the details of her mother's disappearance a second time, culling her vocabulary of words that create ambivalence. *Just. I think. Sorry.*

'She's seventy-three,' she says. 'And it's getting dark.'

'She done it before?' asks the handler.

When Cerys was a child, Margaret would say things like, 'I don't know why I stick around,' or 'You'd be better off without me.' Statements that were always followed by lengthy sojourns in the master bedroom, when Don, Cerys's father, would clear up trays of untouched food from the door.

'No,' says Cerys. 'Never.'

Yet strangely it feels like a lie: as if a specific memory eludes.

'Was there a disagreement?' asks the handler. 'A fight?'

'I just had a baby,' says Cerys.

The handler goes quiet for a while.

'I see. Congratulations,' she says.

Cerys examines herself in the mirror above the sideboard, scrutinising a small freaky mole on her right earlobe. Her mother has the same aberration on her left lobe, a little higher.

'Listen, ring me back if she's not home by midnight, but here's what you should do in the meantime,' says the handler.

Cerys writes down the call handler's recommendations on the back of a utility bill:

Print out a photo of the missing person.

Check bus stops and train stations within a five-mile radius.

Call local A & E departments and enquire about admissions.

Cerys frames the words on the back of the bill with abstract doodles: repeating vine patterns that radiate outwards.

'What about CCTV?' she asks. 'Can you check CCTV?''

'I'd have to open a case, create a crime reference number. From what you've said, it's pretty low risk,' says the handler. 'Call me back if she doesn't show up.'

'The police told me to contact hospitals,' she tells Jim, when he calls half an hour later. 'I printed out a photo.'

'Police? You called the police?'

'She could have fallen. You never know. I've tried ringing a million times now.'

'Police have got better things to do than run about after some crazy pants-suited sociopath,' he says.

Cerys approaches the window and stares at a middle-aged woman rushing down the street towards an Uber.

'She's not a sociopath.'

'It's just attention seeking,' says Jim. 'Maybe narcissistic personality disorder. I'll check the supermarkets.'

'I didn't know you were a psychiatrist,' says Cerys.

'Don't get fucking arsey, ok?'

Cerys steps away from the window as the Uber drives away down the street. As she makes herself a mug of lemon and ginger tea in the kitchen, the mechanics of the task focus her mind, and she remembers a story her cousin Bea shared.

When Margaret was nine years old, her mother Joan disappeared for three months (leaving Margaret with a kindly neighbour). A week later, a vintage postcard from a golf course in Falmouth arrived with the handwritten message: 'Things will be better now I'm gone'.

Seized by restlessness, Cerys paces and wonders whether to phone the police again. What if her mother had the same defective genes as the fugitive Joan? What if this sudden disappearing act was programmed into her from the very beginning: an odd pulsing groove between two strands of DNA?

But when she reaches the hallway, the same sound from the night before echoes beyond the front door: stretched uncertain silences fractured by a progression of hurried footsteps, like some long-forgotten musical cadence. Or Morse code.

Margaret barges through the door carrying several bulging Morrisons bags. A smear of lipstick has coloured the cutting edge of her left incisor tooth; her pants suit is stained with dirt around the hems.

'You were out of formula so—' she says, avoiding Cerys's gaze.

Battling a swirling maelstrom of emotions: rage, guilt, relief, but also a kind of nascent pity, Cerys relieves her mother of the bags and carries them into the kitchen.

'Why you're feeding her yourself god knows,' says Margaret, unveiling a box of formula milk, a glass dropper bottle of gripe water, a dummy.

'Where were you?' asks Cerys.

'I went shopping,' says Margaret. 'I just told you.'

'You were gone for five hours. You cleared your room out.'

'It's all in the boot. I was worried about getting one of those awful anaphylactic shocks,' she says. 'Your guest room is thick with it. Dust. I didn't want it getting on my clothes. Best if I leave first thing in the morning.'

Cerys wants to punch her mother in the tits; stamp over the shopping; suffocate her with the Morrison's Bag for Life. And yet a contrary feeling ripples through her stomach at the same time. As Margaret lines the shopping on the worktop, Cerys wonders what it must have felt like to be a nine-year-old girl waiting for mother to return home. Waiting and then waiting some more. Was it any wonder she was so insecure? Any wonder she viewed her daughter's disregard for the balloon with such mistrust and paranoia? As if it was she who was being discarded and not the balloon. Was it any wonder that she sought to test other people's love for her by taking flight?

'We looked everywhere for you mum. Didn't you get our messages? We contacted the police.'

Margaret's eyes widen to reveal the whites of her eyeballs, as though she's surprised someone bothered to look for her.

'Oh. I expect my phone was out of charge,' she says, almost jovially.

'Jim is still out there. I'll have to ring him,' says Cerys.

'You didn't need to make a fuss.'

A bottle sterilising unit emerges from the final carrier bag. Margaret's fingers tremble as she makes a space for it on a floating shelf above the worktop, as she wipes the gloss surfaces until they shine.

'I'll make you tea,' she says. 'You must be tired'.

Cerys phones Jim from the lounge.

'Guess who's back?'

'Quelle fucking surprise,' he says, after a pause. 'Text me when she goes to bed, I can't face her.'

Margaret, who has changed into an animal-print shirt, tan culottes, suede Chelsea boots, brings in a tray of tea.

'Actually, I need something else from the car,' she says, placing the tray on the sideboard.

'Look mum, you may as well bring in all your stuff from the boot,' says Cerys, hanging up. 'See how it goes. I'll dust the bedroom tonight ok?'

'Oh. The allergy seems to have settled down now,' she says. 'Very odd.'

Cerys listens to her mother leave the house by the front door; the doors of the Volkswagen unlock. A sequence of beeps and other, less identifiable noises reverberate inside Cerys's body like the clattering of her own internal processes. Gathering dirty laundry from the bedrooms, she imagines her mother crumpled in a car crash, her Chelsea boots wedged in her throat: horrible fleeting images she tries in vain to suppress.

'Mum is that you?' she says, when a key turns in the lock minutes later.

'Surprise surprise!' calls her mum.

When she returns downstairs with the laundry basket, Margaret is waiting for her on the sofa in the lounge, with her eyes turned reverentially towards the ceiling.

'It was either this or a blue one with It's A Boy written on it,' she says.

A thirty-two-inch lime green helium balloon, with a blue fin and sludge green markings, clings to a damp patch above the picture rail.

'It's a brontosaurus,' says Margaret. 'Hope you like it better.'

Cerys is confused on so many levels it hurts her head. The brontosaurus was obviously a replacement for the discarded baby girl balloon. But if it was simply a gift, why hadn't her mother brought it in to the house with the shopping? Why had she stowed it in the car? A likelier explanation was that this second balloon was also a test of their love for her: a test they'd passed by going out to look for her. Ergo, they'd earned the balloon.

''Oh,' says Cerys. 'It's very colourful.'

A wide childlike smile spreads across Margaret's face.

'Ultra hi-float technology, that's what the woman in the shop said,' she nods. 'Should last for twelve weeks.'

By the time Jim returns several hours later, the brontosaurus has flipped onto its side. Two dark eye squiggles on one side of its overturned face call to mind the unsettling expression of a primeval sea creature.

'What the actual fuck!' he says.

'Wherever you sit, you can see its eyes,' replies Cerys, whilst feeding Grug. 'It's the Mona Lisa of helium balloons.'

Jim settles on the sofa next to Cerys, setting his travel mug on the floor. A pink streak marks the ridge of his brow.

'You look cold,' says Cerys. 'You ok?''

A similar crescent-shaped streak of pink had appeared on Jim's brow during their expedition to Keepers Pond in Blaenavon, which was also the last time they'd swum together outdoors before the baby.

'Be fine once I've popped that ugly motherfucker,' he says.

'She bought it in Morrisons. Don't touch it. It's got ultra hi-float technology.'

'It looks like a psychotic Marty Feldman,' he says. 'And it's wearing lipstick.'

Cerys erupts with laughter as Jim sips at the remains of his coffee, swearing but then grinning in spite of himself. Finally, they lapse into a prolonged silence punctuated only by sloshing car tyres outside and the baby stirring between sucks.

'Ta for looking,' says Cerys, turning to him suddenly. 'Maybe Grug triggered her abandonment issues.'

'Abandonment issues?'

'Her mother went awol for a few months when she was only a kid.'

'Christ. She should have had my dad,' says Jim. 'Left with his belongings in a bin bag.'

'Sorry,' says Cerys. 'That sounds awful.'

Jim shakes his head and then softly slides his finger along Grug's arm towards her tiny, outstretched palm. A pale rose-pink milk blister has emerged on her top lip from all the sucking.

'You and me Cer, we made a baby,' he says.

Later, as they prepare to go upstairs, the brontosaurus catches their attention.

'Can't help feeling sorry for her though,' says Cerys.

'Why do you always make excuses for her?' asks Jim.

The baffled look on Jim's face reminds Cerys of his expression at Keepers Pond, after she'd swum out further than they agreed, towards an infinity pool at the far end of the pond. He'd hauled her back to shore with his dry bag, worried that she'd developed hypothermia. 'Where were you going?' he'd said. She'd shrugged her shoulders and looked away. Despite later blaming that brief breakout on a moment of disorientation caused by pregnancy, the truth was that the infinity pool had always exerted a pull on her.

'Dunno,' she says. 'Sorry.'

Lifting Grug from the bouncer, Cerys now wonders whether she shares the same perverse, wayward impulses as her mother and grandmother. The same dangerous irresponsible cravings. And yet there is something about this strangely luminous moment in time and space in which all three of them are now immersed that makes Cerys love Jim, and the baby, and her life, more than ever before. It is a love that now bursts outwards from her body, touching everything and everyone.

'I guess I still love her,' she says. 'She's my mum.'

As they reach the landing at the top of the staircase, Grug asleep in Cerys' arms, Jim carrying a glass of water for each of them, a dog-like yelp escapes the spare room, seconds before a dishevelled Margaret appears in the doorway.

'You ok mum?' asks Cerys.

'I forgot to give it to you,' says Margaret, a padded sleep mask propped like sunglasses on her head. 'It wasn't cheap, mind.'

Margaret rummages in her dressing gown as if she's searching for something of utmost importance; as if the object of her search is actually a person; before pulling something from the depths of a satin pyjama pocket. Steadying herself by gripping the door frame with her increasingly arthritic right hand, she leans towards Cerys to hand over her gift: a tiny silver buoy, lustrous and slight, beautifully inscribed with the words 'Balloon Weight'.

'It'll stop it floating away.'

BROAD MONEY

On their way home from school, a little girl asks her mother how much she'd sell her for.

'I'm never going to sell you,' says the mother. 'Don't be silly.'

'Pick a number,' says the little girl, exasperated. 'Any number.'

'I'd never sell you!' says the mother.

The little girl, who is already disappointed by her mother's inability to name the exact colour of the leaves on the path, blows her cheeks out in frustration.

'Please. Just pick a number higher than any number in the world. Like a billion and six.'

The mother stops at the old trailside bollard where the path flattens out. The truth is: she's out of breath. Her cardio-vascular fitness levels are not what they used to be, and life is going at such a hurtling sickening speed that the morning and afternoon of school days have come to feel like nothing more than an in-breath and out-breath. She is also worried that the population of red ladybirds on the bollard has declined.

'Well, some companies have a lot more than a billion and six,' says the mother. 'Amazon. Google. Nestle. So it has to be more than a billion.'

'A trillion and six then?' says the little girl, dropping her school bag into the leaf mulch at the foot of the bollard.

'I still wouldn't sell you,' says the mother. 'Now come on.'

The little girl follows her mother along the path, dragging her school bag like a body, until they are at the bench with the memorial plaque, and foul-smelling telephone kiosk, and the main road that stretches into the city for miles and miles. Watching her, the mother remembers reading an article on the internet that stated that the total sum of money in the world, if you included broad money, meaning all the money in circulation and all digital and theoretical money, was eighty trillion.

'How about eighty trillion and six?' says the mother, finally. 'That could work.'

'Eighty trillion and six is a lot and a lot of money, isn't it?' says the little girl.

The mother nods.

'Ok. I'm going to play now,' says the girl.

god AND THE RuNT

Every night, without fail, Rhidian Reynolds prays for his gran. He prays for a cure for her arthritis and diabetes; he prays she will be happy in the converted dining room; he prays for her border collie, Libby May, in Swansea Dogs Home.

But one night—when he is eleven and three quarters —he forgets.

They find gran's body the following morning after breakfast. Rhidian is in his bedroom memorizing the to-do list in his Ledger of Achievements, when he hears his sister Rachel yelling. Her typically stretched sulky vowels have an odd shrunken quality. Rhidian marks the page in the Ledger and heads downstairs.

The door to the dining room is ajar, framing his mother in profile, who is sitting on the Z-bed clutching a pile of pills. Gran is asleep in the bed, her hand bent across his mother's thigh at such an abnormal angle it reminds Rhidian of those joke hands in the party shop on Craddock Street. Rachel is on the other side of the room, standing between the curtain folds.

'I told her so many times,' says his mother. 'You can't stop the Predsol.'

'I tried waking her,' says Rachel. 'She was freezing cold.'

Rhidian knows what they're thinking but they're wrong. On Tuesday, Gran is taking him to Cranes music shop to buy his birthday present. His heart is set on a red Roland Fantom 8 synthesizer with 88 note keyboard and deep computer integration.

'She's pranking you. She's just pretending,' he says.

Rachel steps out of the curtain folds into a constellation of dust motes. Rhidian catches sight of a mark on her collarbone next to her birthmark. The mark is darker in the middle and around the edges: like the spiral galaxy Andromeda. For a single stretched-out moment, it's as if he's seeing the mark for the first time, when in fact he saw it only yesterday.

'Grow up and quit staring,' says Rachel.

Rhidian stares at the mark on his sister's collarbone, which spins faster and faster as he stares.

'Go to your bedroom Rhid,' says his mother. 'I'll be up later.'

Rhidian climbs the stairs to his bedroom, his mind still fixated on the mark. It had all started when he was cycling home through the cemetery the previous day. He was approaching the slope behind the crematorium, where he liked to freewheel through the angel statues and monkey-puzzle trees, when he heard rustling behind the electricity junction box. Leaning his bike against a privet hedge, he climbed a yew tree to see over the box.

At first, he could only see the basic shape of things: a head, the ridge of a shoulder, legs. But when the shapes assumed substance, he realised that the head belonged to the ginger boy who worked in the crematorium. His name was Barry. Barry Jinks. He was with a girl. Later, as he wrote in his Ledger of Achievements, the scene came back to Rhidian in forensic, Technicolor detail: full of minutiae he wasn't aware of having processed. The boy's hand moving up and down between the girl's legs; the girl's neck twisted sideways to reveal a birthmark; the new mark where the boy had been sucking. The girl—he knew it then – he'd always known it—was his sister Rachel.

Rhidian reaches his bedroom on the top floor, double-checking yesterday's date in the back of the Ledger where he keeps a record of his daily prayers. Gran's full name and address, Violet Amy John, 89 Banwell Street, Swansea, Wales, Earth, the Milky Way, the Universe, the Expanding Multiverse, remains uncrossed, confirming what Rhidian already knows. Last night he'd spent so long praying for his sister—trying to save her from The Unquenchable Fires of Hell – he'd forgotten to pray for his gran.

Setting the Ledger on his desk, Rhidian strikes a deal with Jesus, God, and the Holy Spirit. He will give up his Top Trumps, his Nintendo Switch, one kidney, and the stray cat Tiddles who sometimes visits their garden, in return for his gran. A banging sound, followed by a salvo of smaller bangs, interrupts his thinking.

'I came as fast as I could,' a voice says.

But the voice—small, abject – belongs to his stepfather Alan, not God; the banging nothing more than pipes rattling inside the walls.

'Doctor's gone,' says Rachel, in the hallway sometime later. 'Gran's dead.'

'Could be a coma. You don't know everything,' says Rhidian.

'It was double pneumonia,' says Rachel.

Heidi, Ivy, and auntie Marian pop around in the evening, carrying flowers.

'She forgot the Predsol—she took Warfarin. Two. I'm not sure. I told her and told her—you can't stop it.' Rhidian hears his mother say.

'Shoulda seen Dorothy,' says Heidi. 'Frozen purple she was. Machines everywhere. You got to be grateful.'

Rhidian studies Auntie Marian, who has ear cancer. He spells the word dead over and over in his head. D-e-a-d. D-e-a-d. D-e-a-d.

'She hated it here,' says his mother. 'She'd have been better off staying put.'

Before she became ill, gran lived in a terrace house near Dyfatty Steel Works. With no front garden, there were always people passing by, sticking their noses in. Rhidian thought the converted dining room overlooking the front garden, in a quiet sought-after cul-de-sac, was much nicer.

'She's somewhere better now,' says auntie Marian.

Rhidian watches his mother's nostrils flare, disbelievingly. Rachel picks nail varnish from her fingernails, dropping metallic blue flakes on the carpet like tiny bits of sky. Rhidian is aware of his breathing: the movement of air around his body. A flake of varnish falls on the Velcro straps of his trainers.

'I'm going to the toilet mam,' he says.

In the cloakroom, Rhidian tries to make his eyes see behind the stars, behind the black sky behind the stars, behind the big drop behind the black sky behind the stars. He wants to see God face to face, plead with Him to make everything return to normal. But his eyes won't stretch that far—his mind can't hold it. A knock on the door interrupts his efforts.

'Only me boy,' says auntie Marian.

That night, Rhidian prays harder than he has ever prayed before. He prays as though it's the last time he'll ever pray; as though he has to fit everything into this one single prayer. He rearranges his trophies in order of size on the bookshelf; checks that the valance overhang is equal on either side of the bed; positions the Ledger of Achievements in the precise middle of the bedside table. When he's done, he kneels at his bedside, his head bowed down so far he can feel the ping of his neck cords.

'Our Father, which art in Heaven.'

Already he feels more confident: surprised by his own audacity. If God is his father, surely anything is possible? The rhythms quicken, deepen, transporting him somewhere else: a world of miracles.

'Forgive us our trespasses as we forgive those who trespass against us.'

He stops mid-sentence, realising something. God is giving him a clue, a way of fixing things. A trophy gleams from the shelf like God winking. A shaft of light on the Ledger is like Moses' rod, parting the red sea. Moments later, Rhidian finds himself in his sister's bedroom doorway. God will only listen to him if he forgives Rachel.

'I saw you in the cemetery with that boy,' he says. 'You were being common. Common, coarse and crude.'

The shallow, measured cadences of Rachel's breathing tell Rhidian that his sister is awake, as does the drift of soppy music from her air pods.

'It's your fault gran's dead. I forgot to pray for her because I was praying for you.'

Rhidian pauses before delivering the punchline. He wants his sister to process the depth of her culpability, and by contrast, the power of her brother's awesome grace.

'Good news is I forgive you. So does God.'

Gran's body is already defrosting in Rhidian's mind as he speaks. He pictures her rising to a seated position in the chapel of rest, the power of the Holy Spirit making her hair glow like angels or neon. To distract himself from the jerky sobbing from inside his mother's bedroom, the flatlining of the bin lorries as they reverse into the cul de sac, Rhidian visualizes her size-four feet dangling over the side of the mortuary slab, a pool of pink twinkling meltwater on the floor.

'Get out freak' says Rachel.

Of the funeral, he remembers little except stupid, insignificant details. The undertaker forgets to collect a double spray of white sympathy roses bound with gran's name sash from the florist, which means that they make a detour on their way to the cemetery to pick them up. In the shop doorway, the undertaker rests his hand on the florist's waist. When they reach the cemetery, Rhidian doesn't recognise any of the people waiting on the steps leading to the crematorium. Everything is a blur of black and white shapes moving slowly across the front of the building, like penguins on a rocky coastline. Inside the lobby, gripping the orders of service, is Barry Jinks. Rhidian remembers the way Barry moved his deadly robot arm up and down between Rachel's legs, smashing everything for ever and ever. When they're inside the crematorium, the coffin is balanced on a rickety gurney that looks like a prop; inside the coffin is gran. Rhidian's mind can't accommodate both these observations simultaneously. They contradict each other, cancel each other out. His sister cries but he doesn't. He won't give God the satisfaction.

Rhidian doesn't return to the cemetery at the top of the cul de sac for another fortnight, maybe longer. When he does, the Ledger of Achievements is swinging in a carrier bag hanging from his handlebars, overbalancing the bike.

'Chrissakes watch where you're going!' shouts a man restraining a bull terrier taking a shit by the junction box.

Rhidian imagines kicking a hole in the man's bloated, alcoholic-looking face and then stamping on the terrier's head until its eyes pop out. Ever since the funeral, a black, prickly energy has been surging through the channels of his body, looking for an escape route. He cycles on towards the wheelie bins in the new part of the cemetery, where he plans to dispose of the Ledger.

He has almost reached the Garden of Remembrance when he spots Barry, sprawled across a memorial bench, eating a Ginsters cheese and onion pasty, drinking from a can of Monster. Something about the casual way he's eating the pasty, scattering crumbs on the bench; the way he's swigging from the Monster can indifferently, as though they are not in fact surrounded by dead people, infuriates Rhidian.

'Sign says keep off,' says Barry, when Rhidian's wheels stray onto the grass.

One of the black prickly feelings in Rhidian's belly has reached the root of his lungs. When he sucks it in, it has a heady cleansing effect, like inhaling Vicks. Everything seems clear to Rhidian. There is no one around except for him and Barry Jinks: nothing in the sky except crows.

'Whatever,' he says.

Barry rises from the memorial bench in seeming slow motion.

'What did you say?'

'Why don't *you* keep off?' says Rhidian.

'Fuck's your problem? Runt.'

The fuck comes at Rhidian like a fist; a word of thrilling infinite density like the black hole in his Dorling Kindersley encyclopaedia. Leaning his bike against the bench, Rhidian takes a step towards Barry.

When Rachel discovers Rhidian ten minutes later, having been sent by their mother to look for him, he is lying on the ground, his body straddling the gravel path that leads directly to the Garden of Remembrance.

'Oh my God Rhid! You allright?' she screams.

The fake fur on Rachel's bolero jacket gives her a ghost-like outline that reminds Rhidian of the shape his gran used to make behind the bevelled glass door of their old house, whenever she visited. He remembers jumping into the folds of his gran's woollen pea-green swing coat, into the smell of peppermint creams, and the olden days.

'Something's wrong with the brakes. I was going to phone.'

The details of the fight come back to him slowly as he pulls himself to his feet. Everything had happened so fast, as if to someone else. Barry had shoved him towards the gravel path, the butt of his palm against Rhidian's ribcage. Rhidian had thrust a knee into his groin, at which Barry had bounced backwards as if electrocuted. Then, out of nowhere, blows rained down on either side of Rhidian's head. He felt his skull crack against concrete. At the same time, he'd made something happen. Finally, he'd made something happen.

'You dropped something,' says Rachel, helping him to his feet.

Rhidian glances in the direction of the bulging Aldi carrier bag lying near a dog turd. His Ledger of Achievements.

'Old homework from when I was little,' he says, carrying the bag to a nearby bin.

A clear rain sluices down Rhidian and Rachel's backs as they pass the broken angel statues and twisted monkey-puzzle trees on their way home. Somebody has spray-painted a two-finger peace sign on the junction box.

'It's nobody's fault. About gran,' says Rachel, turning to him.

Rhidian notices how the mark on his sister's neck has faded now, except for a crop of tiny magenta speckles in the centre, like stars in negative. He is aware of his wrists tingling queasily where he was held: the imprint of the ginger boy's palm on his breastbone, as indelible as a tattoo. They are the same now, he thinks, Rachel and him. Both marked and both changed. As they reach the cul-de-sac, he sees his mother hanging up bright triangles of bunting in preparation for his twelfth birthday party the following day. She waves at them from the bay window with a distant, worried, mildly surprised look on her face, like she's waving at unannounced visitors.

'I know that. She just died.'

dEAd iN A gOOd WAY

Everyone should see a dead body. Not the kind of dead body you see in news footage or in films, but a Real Live Dead Body.

The first dead body I saw was dad's. I'd taken mum to see him in a chapel of rest on the other side of town, near to where he grew up. I didn't know what to expect. One of my colleagues told me that they'd draped her mother in a weird nylon thing provided by the funeral home, which they pinned in place around her neck.

'She should have been wearing the pink trouser suit I bought her from Marksies,' she said. 'She looked like the Pope.'

'I'm sorry for your loss,' I said, because what else was there to say.

The undertaker, who had inherited the business from his father-in-law, arranged to meet us in the car park outside the chapel of rest.

'Bonnie's Merc has one of those marvellous built-in sat-navs,' said mum, when a lack of spatial awareness meant I couldn't find the chapel. 'If you'd done medicine like I told you—'

'Bonnie never sees her kids,' I said, interrupting.

My sister Bonnie worked as a solicitor specialising in contract law for some huge shipping company based in Melbourne. Her work schedule meant she couldn't fly over to the UK for another three days.

'Huh. God knows what they'll think of us if we go in late,' said mum, ignoring me.

I parked the Corsa on the main road in front of a nursery school with a hand-painted banner that read 'Don't Be A Fool Don't Park By Our School' draped over the railings. The banner made me feel sentimental and panicky. A building I assumed was the chapel of rest was tucked behind a scruffy line of sycamores further up the road, beyond the road narrowing. The undertaker must have predicted I would have problems finding it, because no sooner had I turned off the engine than he appeared from between the sycamore trees, waving.

'Oh, hi Joy,' he yelled over, as I stepped out of the car. 'You have to drive through the school and around. Didn't they tell you in the office?'

'No,' I said.

'Oh, ok. Well, it should be fine,' he said, approaching.

The undertaker smelled of cheese and a cheap, acidic eau de toilette. His loose-fitting polo shirt seemed odd and inappropriate. I waved at mum to come out of the car.

'Actually I'll stay here,' she said, closing the window. 'I want to remember him as he was, not like a bloody waxwork.'

'You said you needed closure,' I said.

'Spare me the mumbo jumbo!' she said. 'Save it for your clients.'

Ever since I'd quit trying to make a living from photography, I'd worked as a part-time counsellor at a charity for people with mental health problems. Mum had a better solution for my clients. They should count their blessings and/or pull their socks up.

'We could offer a closed casket afterwards, if you prefer,' said the undertaker.

'That could work,' I said. 'Though she might just need a few minutes.'

'I can hear, you know,' said mum.

I walked with the undertaker through a gap in the trees to a tiny car park overlooked by a low-slung building with roughcast render. I tried not to be distracted by the fact that the car park seemed to have no entrances or exits.

'Does he look ok?' I said.

'We left him in the clothes he was in. Colours suited him,' said the undertaker.

'So he looks ok?' I said, again. I was thinking of my colleague's mother and the Pope thing.

'He looks fine all things considered,' he said. 'He'll be behind the door. On your left, as you go in.'

The way he explained it, with his arms mapping out the exact co-ordinates of my dad's corpse, it was as though he was worried I'd get lost again.

'Come out when you've said your goodbyes,' he said.

My father had died really suddenly. One minute he was watching the Six Nations semi-final in the living room with his half-brother Tommy, the next minute he said, 'Oh god,' and closed his eyes. According to Tommy, he didn't say it in shock, or in fear or pain, or even in anticipation, but in the same resigned way he might say 'Oh god' when realising Wales was going to lose.

Since he'd been moved to the chapel from the morgue, Tommy had visited every day, except for one, when he had a hospital appointment for an infusion of iron to stop him falling over on the street. The undertaker's secretary had given him a ballpoint pen fitted with a torch, engraved with Rose Funeralcare.

Mum, meanwhile, hadn't reacted as I thought she would.

'But we're going to Sinah Warren' she said, when Tommy rang her whilst waiting for the ambulance.

She and dad were scheduled to go on a Richards Bros bus tour to The Sinah Warren Hotel on Hayling Island the following weekend. Sinah Warren was one of the few places they both liked. Mum liked the fact it was situated on the site of what was once a 15th century health farm run by monks: perhaps because she had aspirations and liked history. She claimed the air was different on Hayling Island: it cleared her migraines like nowhere else. Dad liked it because he remembered going there as a kid with his four younger brothers when it was a holiday camp.

The day after dad died, mum rung to tell me the trip operators wouldn't give her a refund.

'They offered us an exchange for a trip to Blackpool,' she said.
'Dad's dead, mum,' I said.

'I wouldn't give a thank you,' she said. 'It's a hotspot for crime.'

'I've been to register the death,' I said, because I felt like I needed to hammer it home. The fact that he'd died. 'The doctor recorded myocardial infarction and occlusion of the atherosclerotic coronary artery as the cause.'

'I know that Joy,' she said. 'I'm not an idiot.'

I don't remember the exact moment I pushed the chapel door open and walked in, and I might have stood there for a while, realising I could get away with not going in. Dad wouldn't have cared one iota. He wasn't religious or spiritual. He always said he wanted to be thrown in a skip to save funeral costs, that the Funeral Care Plan he'd paid four thousand pounds into was a "sodding scam."

But as I couldn't stomach more guilt, I went in.

The first thing I remember about the inside of the chapel was that the coffin wasn't behind the door, but in front of me, under an LED crucifix. Also, the chapel seemed bigger on the inside than on the outside, which made me nauseous: as nauseous as I felt looking at the crucifix, which glowed pink and blue and pink. At the same time, I knew I was only experiencing these thoughts because I needed time to process the fact that the feet protruding from the coffin were most definitely dad's feet. He was wearing the Dr Keller orthopaedic slippers I ordered online. I couldn't help but think it was a waste.

I approached the coffin, navigating through rows of chairs that were arranged in a way that left no room for a central aisle. The chairs had foam green seat pads I'd seen in IKEA.

'I won't sleep so …'

It was my mother. Standing by the door. She moved towards me faster than I'd seen her move since the hip surgery a couple of months back.

'Oh. Right. Watch the chairs then!' I said.

'I'm old not bloody blind,' she said.

I didn't look at dad's body until she reached me. After all, it was she who'd seen him first, all those years ago, in the Top Rank in Swansea, in his slim-fitting sport shirt with the double button cuffs, talking to Charlie the doorman. It would have been wrong to deny her the right to be the first to see him again, even if was for the last time in forever.

'Bri!' she howled. She was at the coffin peering in. 'Bri!'

It was a raw analogue sound you could never reproduce digitally, like something being torn from the ground. She leaped back suddenly, waving her arms around.

'Get away from him!' she said.

'What?' I said, thinking she meant me.

'Get it off him!'

A huge bloated thing was buzzing around my dad's body. I removed my scarf to swot it away.

'Get rid of it!' mum said, lunging at the fly. 'Why is it in here!'

'You're gonna fall again,' I said, holding her firmly.

I guided her over to the chairs, which I now noticed were sprayed a preposterous gold colour.

'Get a grip mum,' I said. 'Please.'

After that, I went over to dad, touching his knees and his forehead and his ears, which were red-rimmed from where blood had pooled. I tucked his fingers into the shiny frills of the coffin lining to hide the blackened tips. I took his slippers off. I touched his feet. When Bonnie and I were little, we were afraid of his feet. They were size thirteen and a half, which meant he had to have special shoes made. Every Christmas, he'd create a zig-zagging line of muddy footprints from the fireplace in the best room, to our presents.

'Are Father Christmas's feet a size thirteen and a half too?' we'd say.

'Oh no. He's still only a thirteen! He's still growing!'

After a while, I thought it was probably humiliating for dad to be lying there in his ribbed socks, with a funny stain on his pleated trousers, especially with both of us staring at him, judging how dead he looked. Sweating slightly, I put his slippers back on.

'You ready mum?' I said.

Mum rose and grabbed her stick.

'There's a pie in the fridge that needs eating,' she said, climbing slowly into the car, stopping for breath. 'Come home for lunch. I hate waste.'

'I can't mum,' I said. 'I'm sorry.'

'It's vegetarian. I know how funny you are.'

'It's not that,' I said. 'I've got a client.'

I took the old A road back to work, unable to face the bypass. The street signs, sunk deep into the ground, made the world feel more solid. Mynydd Garnllwyd Rd. Heol Ddu. Sketty Park. But then, as I reached for the radio from inside the glove compartment, it felt as if I was reaching in slow motion for an object far away. I saw myself inserting the radio fascia into the panel, over and over.

I heard mum leave a message on the mobile.

'I'm calling the undertaker's office about the fly,' she said. 'It's not hygienic. It's not right. Ring me when you get in.'

I opened the window for air. I tried to breathe. A little girl and her mother were preparing to cross the road by the traffic lights on the main road. The little girl, who was about seven, was holding a stuffed unicorn. The unicorn fell into the road. The scene reminded me of the cine films dad used to make with his Beaulieu, years ago, not only because I seemed to be watching everything through a strange colorized gauze, but because the speed at which the action took place: the girl bending into the traffic to retrieve the unicorn, the mother yanking her away, her mouth forming a dark ragged hole, all of it was in sync with my delayed sense of perception, allowing me time to fix the moment in memory.

'I will never experience this moment again,' I said to myself. 'I will never ever see dad again.'

As I carried on driving, this intense Super-8 kind of shimmer clung like glitter to everything: the swan-shaped pedalos on the lake outside the university, the old lady pushing her shopper across the overpass, a little boy on a tricycle wearing a helmet and knee pads on the cycle path, his parents running after him, the rain clouds over the Bristol Chanel, moving in. Every single one of them was suddenly so intensely beautiful.

I pulled into the petrol station outside Tesco, parking in the layby with the vacuum and the air, where I cried like a baby and then some. Gathering myself afterwards, I phoned mum.

'I'll pop in after work,' I said. 'I won't be long.'

TREVOR'S LOST GLASSES

My aunt is obsessed with her husband's lost glasses.

'I wake up at four every morning thinking about them,' she says. 'I can't sleep.'

My uncle Trevor lives in a residential nursing home for dementia sufferers. My aunt thinks that one of the care assistants may have pocketed Trevor's glasses and sold them on ebay.

'They weren't cheap,' says my aunt. 'They were over a hundred pounds.'

The glasses have been missing since Christmas. According to my aunt, they were the only pair of glasses that ever suited Trevor's jawline or the shape of his face, and she likes the seam of gold through the sides.

'He looks so handsome in them,' she says.

As far as everybody else in the family is concerned, retrieving the glasses would probably make minimal difference to Trevor's quality of life, since he can no longer read, watch the tele, or recognize faces. Recently he has started to gnaw on people's fingers when he's hungry.

'Maybe bring him his old ones?' I say. 'The silver ones.'

My aunt reacts as if I'm suggesting that she gift him a big bag of shit, raising her upper lip to expose her teeth.

'At least it's something Audrey,' I say.

My aunt eventually succumbs to the idea of the silver glasses. But the angles of Trevor's face must have warped since the time he last wore them, because when my aunt brings them in to the home, the square frames only emphasise the drooping of his brow, the expanding sink holes of his eye sockets.

'He looks like a *duwelp*,' says my aunt.

'Duwelp' is a phrase derived from the Welsh word for God, which is Duw, and the word 'help'. As in *God help them*. My aunt has noticed more 'duwelps' than ever before, especially at the bus stop and in Wetherspoons.

'Show him the memory book,' I say. 'You never know.'

My aunt pulls out the memory book from the drawer in Trevor's nightstand, turning to the first spread of photos. Trevor snatches the book from his wife and begins to chew on it, adding to the existing teeth marks along the spine and on the corners. Dissatisfied, he tilts the book up to his face, before suddenly pausing mid-way. Slowly, precisely, he traces the outline of a figure in the photograph with his finger, as if he's tracking a line in a maze. His mouth opens and closes like a fish.

'That's your mam,' says my aunt. 'And that's you.'

Trevor pulls the book closer and closer, applying it to his face like one of those soothing hot flannels you get on planes.

'You're in the back garden by the cherry blossom. Think you were about ten.'

'No, no!' he shouts, suddenly irate as he throws the book down. 'It was a pear tree. One of two. It stopped making pears when I was five. Summer before I started school. There were white flowers and what not, and then nothing. Then there was the war. I don't know what happened.'

My aunt bends down to retrieve the book, hovering curiously in mid-stance for a while. When she finally comes up, as if for air, I can see she's been crying.

'Oh Trev. I miss you something awful,' she says.

After that incident, my aunt is determined to find Trevor's lost glasses.

'It's the first time he's spoken in months,' she says. 'Imagine the difference the old ones will make.'

My aunt removes Trevor's clothes from the wardrobe, turning out the pockets of a three-piece suit that's been sealed in a dry-cleaning bag ever since he moved into the home. ('You never know, they might have a party or a dinner or a special guest,' my aunt had said when she hung the suit on the railing.)

'They won't be in the suit Audrey,' I say. 'He's never used it.'

'They're nothing but a bunch of good for nothing wasters,' she says, meaning the care assistants.

The following week, my aunt pins a large blurry photo of my uncle wearing his original glasses to the noticeboard in the lobby, the words 'Have you seen these glasses?' scrawled in Sharpie beneath.

A small bird-like resident called Joan, who is always in the hallway, or in the lobby, watches on.

'Give me that pen,' she says afterwards. 'I need to write my mother a letter to explain things.'

Meanwhile, under duress from my aunt, the nursing home manager organizes a visit from a local optician, who duly prescribes a third pair of glasses.

'Wish I'd been there,' says my aunt, when the glasses arrive a week later, enclosed in a small grey pouch at the bottom of an oversized Amazon cardboard box. 'I don't like them.'

The new glasses have large square transparent frames and thick bottle-cap lenses. The wires and inner workings are all visible.

'He looks like a bloody bug in them,' says my aunt.

'The high index lenses were much more expensive,' says the nursing home manager, defensively. 'The optician said it wouldn't make a difference. Said his prescription is so high now that there was only so much they could thin down the lenses.'

'It makes a difference to me,' says my aunt. 'I'm his wife.'

The lost glasses turn up in the end. Discovered in the room of a resident from the high dependency wing housed in a new block in the car park. A ginger eyelash belonging to the resident, a man called Don Jenkins from Treboeth, is found stuck between the rim and the lens. My aunt tugs at the lash with her freshly shellacked fingernails.

'All that waiting and now this,' says my aunt, flinging the glasses on to the bed. 'It's all too bloody much, Chrissy.'

'I know. I'm sorry.'

Picking up the glasses from the bed, I polish each lens with my cardigan, pulling the lash out with my Tweezerman. Later, when I ease them on to my uncle's head, over the crumbling red rims of his ears, into the ready-made ridge on his nose, I realise that whilst he definitely looks better in these glasses, he looks nothing like the Trev I once knew.

'There,' I say.

A care assistant walks into the bedroom carrying instant coffees, tea in a beaker, three slices of thickly-cut Swiss roll. Trevor picks at an invisible piece of lint on his jumper, ignoring the assistant, and us.

'Oooh. If only I were a little older Trev!' says the care assistant, laughing coyly at her own joke. 'You look so handsome! Lucky Audrey!'

My aunt turns away towards the window. In a small garden opposite the nursing home, a woman in her forties is unpegging laundry from a clothesline: a man's trousers, children's socks, a red flowing dress that seems too young for her. The sky is this weird, extra-terrestial amethyst colour, sheeted with incoming rain.

'Actually, no tea for me today, Shelley, thank you. It's gonna rain. I got things on the line.'

My aunt picks up her handbag like it's a weight, even though it contains nothing but a comb, pocket tissues, and a purse. She rummages through the compartments of the purse, zipping, unzipping haphazardly.

'Bloody bus pass, must have dropped it,' she says.

'Niall is picking up the kids from school,' I say. 'I can drive you home if you want?'

'I keep on losing everything,' says my aunt, looking down.

The care assistant, who is hunched down beside Trevor, brings the beaker of tea to Trevor's mouth. Steam mists the lenses of Trevor's glasses, forming rising columns of altocumulus clouds that obscure his eyes, and I figure that maybe the main difference between this Trevor and the old Trevor is not the glasses nor the drooping of his face, but the fact that you can't tell what this Trevor is thinking. (Which is perhaps not as bad as believing that you know what a person is thinking, when basically you don't have a clue, which is almost definitely the case with most people.)

'You haven't lost Trevor, Audrey,' I say. 'He's in there, he's just stuck.'

The care assistant, who smells of tropical body mist, powdered milk, and something else, places a mug of strong tea on the nightstand beside my aunt, briefly resting her hand on my aunt's shoulders.

'I already poured you one, Audrey,' she says. 'May as well drink it while it's hot.'

PAiN
SLuTS

Elaine has begun to fantasise about a double mastectomy. In the fantasy, a surgeon places a frame across the top of Elaine's body, which he drapes with a pastel blue sheet. Then, with two dismissive flicks of his wrist, he removes Elaine's breasts. Elaine sees only the result. A flat uncluttered chest stripped of everything except the essentials.

'You should learn to love your body,' says Elaine's friend Liz, when they meet at the M&S café one afternoon. 'Did I tell you about Rose?'

'Yes Liz,' says Elaine. 'Many times.'

Rose is Liz's grandmother-in-law. Back in the spring, Liz had accompanied her new husband William to Nigeria to meet his family. Whilst Liz was enjoying a barbecue with William's family, Rose pulled a chair alongside them, wresting a withered eighty-year-old tit from her blouse. Liz was so taken aback by the beauty of Rose's blouse (a retro Burberry print overlaid with polka dots), it took her several seconds to register the breast.

'She said it was a tradition for new family members to suckle on elders,' says Liz, retelling the story.

'It was a prank though, right?' says Elaine.

Liz draws up breath through her nostrils.

'Yes. But at least she wasn't ashamed of her breasts.'

Elaine isn't ashamed of her breasts. Neither does she have breast cancer like her friend Rhiannon. Elaine's breasts have simply outgrown their relevance and purpose, and seeing them sends vague twinges of sadness and desperation through the rest of her body.

'I'm not ashamed. I just don't want them,' says Elaine.

On the way back from her catch-up with Liz, Elaine buys a sports bra from Bravissimo: a forty-five-pounds white number with high-impact compression fabric.

'I've got one in blue, one in indigo,' says the woman at the till. 'Once you get the hang of the fiddly bits it's super comfy.'

Elaine is not looking for comfort. Elaine is looking for a contraption that will quash not only her tits but her feelings too. Recently she read an article in National Geographic about breast ironing: a procedure in which young women got their breasts pounded with grinding stones to stop them growing.

'Thanks. I can't wait,' says Elaine.

By the time she gets home, the sports bra is burrowing into Elaine's ribs and armpits. The hook and eye claw at her vertebrae; the straps dig in like cheese wire.

Ordering another three of the same bras online, Elaine wonders whether similar solutions exist for all of her superfluous body parts.

Her pointless clit. Her pointless ass. Her pointless hair.

The following day, when she visits the hairdresser—not the salon in the regenerated Marina she usually frequents but an older ladies' salon called Paradox—Elaine asks for a Grade One haircut.

'You mean a pixie cut?' says Trish, who has squared-off coffin nails in various colours. 'I can tease out the roots to give you volume.'

Under the sports bra, the prickly sensation in the innermost part of Elaine's right breast has joined up with a similar sensation in her left breast to form a continuous band of black-red pain. She can barely breathe, let alone talk.

'No, a skinhead,' she says.

Trish's perplexed expression forces Elaine to qualify her statement.

'I'm starting chemo,' she lies.

'I'm so so sorry love,' says Trish. 'Can I get you a tea?'

Elaine's guilt over the lie reconstitutes itself as a pained off-centre smile. When the hairdresser's mouth continues moving, Elaine nods in agreement, even though she doesn't hear a single word.

All she can think about is her friend Rhiannon who begins chemo on Monday.

'I want to cut it before it falls out.'

'What the hell have you done?' says Liz, when they meet in the Debenhams espresso bar later that day. 'I'm worried about you.'

Elaine sees her reflection in the window. The texture of her hair makes her think of a Fuzzy Felt board. As a child, Elaine once owned a Fuzzy Felt craft box called Felt Fantasy. The box contained numerous felt shapes in shades of lime, pink, and yellow. There were stick-on googly eyes that could be combined to create startled-looking creatures from outer space.

'It was getting on my fucking nerves,' she says.

Before the scalping, Elaine's hair was crafted as a feathered two-toned bob that cost seventy-five pounds every six weeks to maintain.

'It was always lovely Elaine. I don't know what you're talking about.'

Elaine focusses in on Liz's equally expensive Anna Wintour-style lob; the tailored shirt with dangling pussy bow; the braided scarf that reminds her of a tampon string. Too much, she thinks. Lose the scarf. She thinks about Liz's gran-in-law plucking a nipple from her blouse like a magic trick.

Elaine's nipples are meanwhile killing her. She wouldn't be surprised if they were gangrenous: if they fell to the floor like frozen warts. She imagines feeding her nipples to her cat Orlando as a treat.

'How's William?' she says to Liz, requiring distraction.

'Starts a project in Canada in a month. Least I'll have the house to myself.'

Through the espresso bar's wraparound windows, Elaine watches everyone rush for cover from the sudden rain.

'You should go with him,' Elaine blurts. 'Canada gets top marks on all those happiness quality-of-life thingummyjigs. What have you got to lose?'

Liz peers at Elaine with her mouth wide open, revealing a forest of fillings.

'I have work,' says Liz. 'Remember?'

'It's an opportunity, that's all,' says Elaine.

Elaine buys herself a new wardrobe of inconspicuous unisex clothing. White button-down shirts from M&S Classics (three quarter sleeves to hide her dangling upper arms); structured black and grey jeggings from Debenhams. To protect herself from the disgusted prurient stares of all the younger people, she also buys a pair of smoke lens, oversized sunglasses.

When she tries on the final item, a Spanx body suit designed to flatten the mound of her groin, she is blindsided by a new pain that tears through her collarbone like wildfire.

'You ok?' says an assistant, from beyond the curtains. 'Thought I heard something.'

Inside the dressing room, Elaine is on her knees on the floor, clutching a stool that's toppled over. The body suit stretches all the way from the bottom of her thighs to her ribs, squeezing flesh through an opening beneath the sports bra.

'I'm coming in,' says the assistant, opening the curtains.

Elaine has never hated herself quite so much as she does now. But when the assistant helps her up by the hand, Elaine doesn't want to let go.

'Can I call someone?' says the assistant, pulling her hand away.

Elaine breathes in slow and hard.

'I'm quite alright. Thank you.'

Elaine lies on her bed in the nude, allowing herself some time to rest. After the humiliation of the changing room (the assistant zeroing in on her overhang, the icky limp clamminess of her flesh), Elaine decides that she will no longer dare to venture out without the shapewear.

Setting the timer on her phone, Elaine's eyes drift towards the damp patch on the ceiling.

The night before her husband Dan had left, the radiator in the ensuite sprung a leak. 'Who knew there was so much water in the house?' Dan had said, when they used up all the bath towels. By the time the water stopped, it was four in the morning. With a strange asymmetrical drooping of his cheeks, Dan had made his way to the spare bedroom to sleep. When Elaine went to check on him in the morning he was gone. 'I can't do it anymore,' said the note.

As Elaine reaches for her sleep mask from the bedside table, a pre-scheduled alarm blares abruptly and she scrabbles across the floor to find the phone, dugs dangling downwards like a cow's. Had she fallen asleep? Where was her self-control? Staggering back to bed, phone in hand, a breeze from the bedroom window suddenly steals across her abdomen and chest.

Her breasts are abnormally cold. Cold as witches' teats. Cold that is concentrated around her nipples, forming circles that map the circumference of her areolae, as if the area has been sprayed in liquid nitrogen. Touching her nipples to inspect, Elaine discovers that the coldness is actually moisture, cooling and evaporating on her skin.

It was impossible of course: she was fifty. Twenty years had passed since she last breast-fed Gareth. And yet the accompanying tingling in her breasts is the same. In the darkness of her bedroom, Elaine licks her dripping fingers to check.

'Promise me you'll get yourself checked?' says Liz, when Elaine shares her news. 'It's not normal.'

'I googled it. Excessive breast and nipple stimulation causes lactation.'

'You could be ill,' says Liz. 'You're fifty-one.'

'Fifty. And I'm fine. It was the sports bra.'

Elaine sips the last of her spiced pumpkin latte autumn special before excusing herself to go use the toilet. In the disabled cubicle, as the milk speeds through ducts into her nipples, Elaine pops a breast pad in her bra. The way Elaine sees it, she has brought her breasts back to life. She is the Dr Frankenstein of tits but in a good way. This morning, she hauled a heavy crate of maternity accessories down from the attic like superwoman.

'Rhiannon finished chemo,' says Liz, when Elaine returns to their table. 'She just texted.'

Liz slips into a cropped apple green jacket made of boucle fabric with a fleshy rose corsage on her breast pocket.

'They shrunk the tumour. I said we'd go see her.'

'Brilliant news,' says Elaine.

Rhiannon is waiting for them in her open plan family room, a bright orange scarf wrapped around her head like an elaborate turban.

'Fuck have you done to your hair?' she says to Elaine.

Elaine feels her jowls flushing red.

'It was getting on my bloody nerves. I looked like the Grand High Witch.'

'If you ever change your mind, my hair's in a shoe box in the den,' says Rhiannon.

Elaine recalls the locks of Gareth's baby hair stuffed in a jewellery box on her dressing table; the hospital band from his tiny wrist curled in a commemorative mug; his baby teeth, somewhere. She hasn't seen Gareth, who lives in Edinburgh, for months.

'It's good news about the tumour though, right?' Liz says to Rhiannon, reaching for a slice of lemon drizzle cake. 'When's the lumpectomy?'

Rhiannon adjusts the front of her turban.

'I'm getting a tattoo,' she says. 'I'm going flat.'

A crumb from the drizzle cake tumbles into Liz's cleavage. Elaine suppresses a strange urge to fish for the crumb with her tongue.

'What do you mean 'going flat'?' says Liz. 'I don't know what you mean.'

Rhiannon flips her smartphone out towards them. Frozen on the screen is an unknown woman, and across her chest, where there would have been breasts, is a tattoo.

'Whip them off,' says Rhiannon.

The tattoo is magnificent. Huge. A trail of hyper-real cherry blossom that caresses the contours of the unknown woman's body, sweeping over her chest and down her side.

'It's stunning,' says Elaine.

Liz gives Elaine a dirty look.

'Not sure that's helpful Elaine.'

'If it's what Rhiannon wants,' says Elaine.

Liz walks over to the bi-fold French doors, which open on to a graveled walkway and a steep flight of steps leading to the rest of the garden. Trees partially obscure the view of the municipal cemetery and crematorium smokestack beyond the cul-de-sac.

'This is crazy,' says Liz, with her back to them.

A neatly arranged row of plastic bags, pegged to the washing line, distracts Elaine from the fact that Liz has begun crying.

'I'm so sorry Liz,' says Rhiannon, rushing to comfort her. 'It's stressful for everyone.'

'It's not your fault,' says Liz. 'It's the whole situation.'

Elaine joins them at the door, resting her head on Liz's shoulder.

'We should do something nice when this is over.'

Back at home, Elaine sits by the window to pump her milk. Shifting her position in the armchair so that the arm supports her lower back, she attaches the pump's suction cup to her breast.

Something about the light, the position of the bottle on the armchair, the way the milk gushes out of her bosom like water, makes it seem as if no time has passed at all: as if Gareth is in his buggy in the hallway, as if Dan is at the office.

Elaine tries not to move.

If she moves the illusion will end.

But as soon as she's inched herself into optimal position a postman appears on the path outside, fumbling in his postbag. The slap of the letter box flap, the rustle and slide of mail landing on the tiles, out of sync with the postman's movements and position, shatters Elaine's concentration.

Elaine carries her breast milk to the kitchen. The phone rings as she rinses bottles.

'Come with me to the tattooist,' says Rhiannon. 'I've got a consultation.'

The tattoo parlour is in one of the Victorian arcades in Cardiff.

'You still a hundred percent sure about this?' says Elaine, as they're directed to a waiting room out back.

'Should have done it years ago,' says Rhiannon. 'When I discovered I had the gene.'

'No, the tattoo,' says Elaine.

'Fucking chemo melts your brain,' laughs Rhiannon, a little sourly. 'I poured milk in the kettle this morning.'

As if on cue, milk seeps through Elaine's breast pads to her shirt, forming an inchoate shape like a continent. She zips up her jacket to hide the stain. The wine on the train has made her feel sick.

'You ok?' says Rhiannon.

'I'm a bit cold,' says Elaine.

'Actually you're pretty hot!' says Rhiannon, laughing.

Elaine is too focussed on not being sick to engage in Rhiannon's weird banter. A man with sideburns stretching to the side of his mouth emerges from behind a metal door to call for Rhiannon.

'If you don't mind, I'll wait here,' says Elaine.

By the time she gets home from the trip Elaine's breasts feel like red-hot viscous spheres straight from the earth's core. Pain is part of the process of transformation, she tells herself. Taking three co-codamols washed down with Chardonnay, she uses the breast pump from Mothercare to ease the pressure in her tits. The new £107 double pump features two modes and six suction levels, allowing Elaine to pump both breasts simultaneously.

Skipping the slower rhythms of the 'Letdown Phase,' Elaine switches straight to 'Expressing Mode'. The suction reminds her of the love bites Dan once gave, back in those early days: on the nape of her neck, in the groove of her armpits.

Elaine increases the suction power. When she turns to alleviate the pressure on her back, the buzzing of the pump gives way to a louder more urgent rat-tat-tat noise. Out of nowhere Liz appears in the window: the visceral horror on her face triggering Elaine's fight or flight.

Elaine rushes to the kitchen with the pump. She dumps it in

the sink under a chopping board. When she finally opens the front door, Liz is holding out a bunch of tulips.

'Rhiannon said you weren't well. Said you missed the consultation.'

'It was just a headache,' says Elaine. 'I'm fine.'

'You're not fine,' says Liz.

Elaine takes the tulips to the kitchen, freeing them from their plastic wrapper. Swinging the tap away from the cargo of evidence in the larger sink, she fills a vase with water.

'You have to stop all this nonsense, Elaine,' says Liz.

Elaine slashes the tulip stems lengthwise to resurrect them.

'You look drained. Like a ghost.'

'Ironically it's given me a new lease of life,' says Elaine. 'I feel like a million dollars. Like Helen Mirren on speed.'

'Right. And what are you going to do with all the milk?'

Elaine considers the dated sandwich bags full of breast milk stuffed in the freezer. She's been meaning to contact the milk bank at the hospital.

'I'm going to drink it,' she says. 'It's a superfood.'

A delivery lorry reverses into the lane behind Elaine's house with its back-up beeper blaring. Elaine pops the tulips into the vase and walks them over to the table where Liz is sitting. The words had escaped her involuntarily, without warning.

'What the fuck happened to us?' says Liz.

Elaine drags a chair over to Liz who is crying. She hands her some pocket tissues from the sideboard.

'I'm not sure why I said that,' says Elaine.

Liz laughs darkly and wipes her eyes, smearing mascara over her face. Elaine not only regrets the comment about drinking the breastmilk, she regrets being a terrible friend, and a worse human being. At four a.m. she had a flashback to the hairdressers and her lie about the chemo.

'You look like a deranged raccoon,' says Elaine, tucking a strand of hair behind her friend's ear. 'I'll make you tea.'

'Wine, obviously,' says Liz.

By the time Elaine has finished pouring them each a wine, Liz has used all the pocket tissues to remove the rejuvenating caviar foundation she uses. The bare blotchy skin of her face looks like the 'Before' pictures in all those celebrity magazines.

'I quit my job by the way,' she says. 'Told Lester where to shove his appraisal.'

Liz works as an office manager for a recruitment agency. It was meant to be a temporary arrangement, after she moved from London to look after her mother fifteen years ago.

'At long fucking last,' says Elaine. 'You hated that bloody job. You can go to Canada now.'

Liz pulls a small velvet pouch from her bag, shaking her head.

'I'm starting a business on Etsy,' she says, emptying the pouch on the table. 'Brooches, corsages, headbands, handmade by yours truly.'

'Oh,' says Elaine. 'That's amazing.'

Orlando jumps onto the table, rubbing his flank against Elaine's shoulder. The tinkle of his collar bell is as remote as wind rushing through sail masts.

'I made you a lace choker.'

Elaine tries the choker in the mirror, which is constructed from delicate grey macrame with a strip of leather weaved through. Elaine imagines being led around the living room on a lead attached to the choker.

'It's sweet,' says Elaine.

The following morning Elaine takes a walk around town. The new extra-tight sports bra that she ordered online is coiled around her ribcage like a python; the taste of breastmilk lingers in her mouth. After Liz left her house the previous evening, Elaine had transferred her breast milk into a maxi-sized feeding bottle, drawing up five millilitres into a syringe. Confident it would accelerate her transformation, she expelled the contents of the syringe onto a spoon.

But the milk had tasted stronger than expected. Pooled like liquid mercury on her tongue. She'd thrown the rest down the sink and gone to bed.

In the Kardomah cafe, where she and Rhiannon have arranged to meet, Elaine takes a seat by the open door. A waitress brings

Elaine's skinny decaf latte to the table (with a glass of hydrating tap water), her dinner-lady arms flapping against Elaine's cheek.

'What happened to the turban?' says Elaine, when Rhiannon arrives. 'I didn't recognise you.'

Rhiannon has exchanged her turban for a platinum wig that Elaine worries is *too* wiggy. A slogan on her T-shirt reads I'VE GOT CANCER. WHAT'S YOUR EXCUSE?

'I got my hair made into a wig and then they dyed it,' says Rhiannon. 'I was tempted to go old-lady-purple.'

'They can do that?'

Rhiannon leans over the table, turning the side of her head towards Elaine.

'Touch it,' she says. 'Feels like silk.'

Elaine strokes the side of Rhiannon's hair like she's stroking the upper atmosphere of a planet, like she's afraid of going deeper, making contact.

'Christ knows what they've done to it,' says Rhiannon.

Elaine parts some strands and dips a finger in, holding her breath. It was a while since she'd touched another person, or been touched, unless you counted the smear test nurse, the mammogram nurse, and the hairdresser. Even so, it was embarrassing to be touching her friend's hair, in public, in this café. Especially at their age. In their state. It would put the diners off their lattes and cake.

'It's lovely,' she says, pulling away.

'What the matter?" says Rhiannon. 'You seem distracted.'

The chequered black and white pattern on the Formica table pulses to the same beat as Elaine's breasts. For a while now, Elaine has wanted to tell Rhiannon about the sports bras, how she's been grinding her bits down with shapewear. If it weren't for the breast cancer, she'd have done so already. The altercation with Liz has made it urgent.

'I bought some sports bras to squish down my tits,' she says. 'Then last week I started lactating. I told Liz I was going to drink my own breast milk.'

Rhiannon takes a bite of a pastry, as if nothing unusual has been said.

'Your tits are magnificent,' she says. 'Remember that spa day in the Gower? The communal changing rooms. I couldn't stop looking at your areolae.'

Light filters through the arcing leaves of several palm trees perched by the café window, bathing Rhiannon's skin in a silver otherworldly radiance.

'They look like they've been chewed by a dog,' says Elaine. 'Like they've been chewed up then spat out then stood in.'

Rhiannon licks jam from her fingers.

'Shut up and come with me.'

Elaine follows Rhiannon down some gilded art deco staircase to the disabled cubicle at the back of the café like they're teenagers about to do drugs.

Rhiannon takes her clothes off in the cubicle.

'I like to pee and poop in the nude,' she says. 'It's liberating.'

'Liberating and freezing,' says Elaine.

Elaine stares at her friend's naked body as she pees. It appals her to think that one day soon, Rhiannon's breasts will be flung into one of those yellow hospital wheelie bins as waste. Anatomical garbage. Even so, at that precise moment in time, her friend's breasts are still beautiful, with small frosted pink nipples.

Rhiannon wiggles her hips to drip dry before pulling on her knickers. When she buttons her blouse, something short circuits in Elaine's body. There is a dim kind of throbbing at the root of her left nipple and then nothing. She would like to get her tits out to check that they're still there. She would like to show them to Rhiannon once more.

'I've been a twat,' says Elaine. 'I'm really sorry.'

'Cancer's a total mindfuck,' says Rhiannon.

Rhiannon plants a kiss on her cheek: a wet, sweet, perfumed kiss that takes a long time to dry.

'I wanted to show you something,' she says. 'Cheapskate ink cartridges, but what do you think?'

Rhiannon plucks a rolled-up sheet of A4 from her bag and flattens it on the lid of the toilet cistern. Lines of loose toner ink obscure the printed image of a woman. Elaine digs her new varifocals from her tote bag and brings the print-out to her face.

Across the woman's chest is another mastectomy tattoo. More radical, more beautiful, than the cherry blossom.

'The artist is in New York,' says Rhiannon. 'You and Liz should come with me.'

Elaine takes the coastal road home, detouring through the open grasslands of Fairwood Common. As a teenager, the common was Elaine's favourite part of the peninsula. A blank space between two villages that seemed to go on for ever. A place where, for the duration of time it took you to drive from one end of the common to the other, you could be anybody or anything you wanted. (If there was time, you could be more than one thing). Pulling into a bus stop beyond Lunnon, Elaine tugs the sports bra through her sleeve and rings Liz.

'Rhiannon invited us to New York,' she says, when Liz answers. 'The tattoo artist she wants lives in Brooklyn. I'm guessing it would be some time in the Spring. After the surgery.'

'So, she's definitely doing it?' says Liz. 'The tattoo?'

Elaine pulls down the boned, spandex thigh cincher beneath her pencil skirt, releasing herself finally, fully, from the hideous death grip of the shapewear. The angel tattoo that Rhiannon had shown her in the café was the most beautiful piece of art Elaine had ever seen, full of dark, inky flickerings. One third angel, one third armour, one third bird, the more she'd stared at the image, the more it seemed as if the wings were drying and hardening in preparation for flight, as though the woman in the photograph was changing form. A sudden pain had taken hold behind Elaine's own breasts: at first, she assumed it was wind. But the pain was more complex than wind, closer to her heart, a series of scrabbling, creaturely sensations, as if something was trying to break out of her body. Leaving the car now, with her phone in hand, Elaine bundles the shapewear into a bin next to the bus stop.

'Elaine? You still there?' asks Liz.

'Yes,' says Elaine. 'She's still doing it. Change is good.'

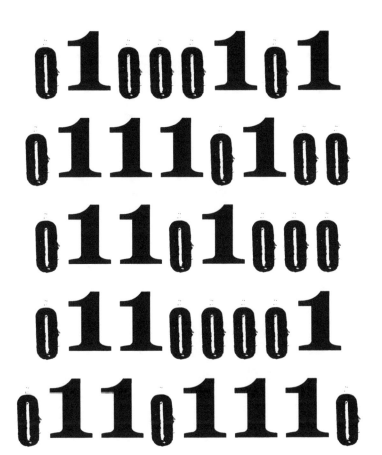

The Hopkins family are enjoying a picnic at a half-broken trestle table near the edge of a forest when nine-year old Ethan suddenly stands.

'When I'm thirty-five, daddy will be dead,' he says.

His sister's powder blue eyes judder like a computer glitch.

'Don't say that!' she screams.

Ethan is bemused by Cadi's response, the jerky eye action, the drama. He only said it because he loves figuring out the math of all things. The math of people. The math of life. The math of death. There is only a one in three hundred trillion chance of being born. Ninety-nine point nine nine nine nine nine nine nine percent of a person's body is empty space. If the age of the universe is a year, humans would only appear for the last twenty seconds. These are his favourite facts.

'Men live until they're 81 years old and daddy was 46 when I was born.'

Over the Whitsun half-term, Ethan is learning dinosaur names in binary code. He enjoys reducing things down to ones and zeroes; the numbers help his stomachaches dissolve. The binary code for the largest ever carnivorous dinosaur, Spinosaurus, is 01010011 01110000 01101001 01101110 01101111 01110011 01100001 01110101 01110010 01110101 01110011. Soon he will finish memorising the code for Ichthyosaurs, the biggest aquatic dinosaur, and the code for Quetzalcaotlus, the biggest flying dinosaur. In binary code his own name, Ethan, is 01000101

01110100 01101000 01100001 01101110, which makes him feel almost as cool as a dinosaur.

'Shut it, dweeb,' screams Cadi.

Ethan's older sister, Ella, who is lying on a picnic blanket a few feet away, removes her air pods and looks over. NWA lyrics stream through the crisp, late Spring air towards them.

'Wow. Heartless, bro,' she says.

She speaks with a drawly accent gleaned from countless hours of watching The End of the Fucking World, pronouncing 'heartless' as two distinct and drifting syllables that give it a terrible, almost literal quality. Ethan is baffled by how she heard him.

'I'm not heartless,' he says, his lower lip quivering.

'It wasn't nice, Ethan, that's all,' says his mother, who suddenly remembers a story she read recently about a baby born with his entire still-beating heart protruding from a split in his sternum. 'Daddy will live longer than that. He'll be back on Friday. We can go out for dinner.'

Ethan swings his leg over the broken picnic bench and heads towards the trunk of a fallen oak that sits beside a stream and a curiously shaped Iron Age garbage mound. His shoulders droop. He doesn't run. When he finally arrives at the tree trunk he simply stands there with his back to them. From the the way his arms hang, like deflated windsocks, his mother knows that he's crying.

'I found the pepperami sticks you were looking for,' she says, walking over to him. 'They were in the other carrier bag. And I've got the secret ingredient cupcakes you like. C'mon, forget it now, baby.'

'Ella said I'm heartless,' he says, like it's a question.

'Of course you're not heartless,' she says.

The mother, who also likes math, especially algebraic geometry, makes a fist with her son's soft and grubby fingers, lifts it to the centre of his chest, and presses it into the valley between his lungs.

'Your heart beats over a hundred thousand times a day,' she says. 'Go on. Feel it.'

Ethan closes his eyes to do the math. Behind the gauzy pink skin of his eyelids, his eyeballs twitch like the spectral silhouettes of dancers behind a screen, and his mother wonders, not for the first time, whether existence requires physicality, or whether mathematical objects exist independent of our conception of them. She now veers towards the notion that even though we can't see, taste, feel, or smell numbers, they might, indeed, exist.

'That's 36,500,000 times a year,' says Ethan.

'Over a billion times in a single lifetime,' says his mother.

The mother tousles the whorls of Ethan's hair and teases out a tiny louse. When she snaps the louse dead between her fingernails, a speck of Ethan's blood escapes its pale and bloated body, and her insides churn over with a mix of love and anxiety and then some. Ethan burrows his head into the soft of her belly.

'I miss daddy,' he says.

dEATh AND THE TEENAGE STRiPPER

Rachel steps into the bay of her bedroom window. The windowpane is streaked with seagull shit and skeins of dirt from the crematorium smokestack, but all that matters to Rachel is that the funeral-goers see her strip.

Steadying herself in the window, she checks her phone again. 9.40am. Almost time. But no sooner has she angled her half-naked body towards the hearse, a big-assed Mercedes E-class, than the sound of footsteps on the upstairs landing stops her dead.

'There's stuff to go on the line,' yells Fay.

The idea of being caught, mid-strip, by her mother, makes Rachel want to douse herself in acid.

'Mam. I'm changing. Don't come in!'

But Fay is in the doorway already, reflected in the dressing table mirror opposite the bedroom door. Their perspectives meet now on the underwear, strewn across the carpet like petals. A padded balcony bra with sequins like moon crescents, knickers with their gussets turned out. Rachel flings her arms around her chest.

'That's what you're changing into is it?' says Fay.

Rachel stuffs the underwear into the back of her wardrobe on top of last year's A cups. Downstairs, her mamgu Violet starts coughing, launching a stream of rippling air fronts that swirl though the house in ever widening circles.

'I've got to see to mamgu,' says Fay. 'I want you down in five minutes.'

Fay is standing next to the Whirlybird washing line behind the shed when Rachel finally reaches the garden, the blue of her sweater like a shred of tethered sky. She doesn't mention the episode in the bedroom.

'Old sheets first,' she says.

On the line are rows of sheets and old people's clothes. The best items are on show on the outside, whilst the older ones, gaunt-looking winceyette nightgowns, faded candy-stripe bedlinen, long johns, droop like bats from the innermost line. Sheets flap against Rachel's body as she works, reminding her of the macrame lace curtain across the door of her mamgu's old house. Working outwards from the centre of the washing line, it's as though she's moving not only through space but also time.

'Don't want them getting dirty again,' says Fay. 'Be smoky in no time.'

The smokestack is already sending scribbles of smoke into the sky. Rachel remembers how, early in the summer, before she'd started performing the stripteases in the window, a piece of grit landed in her eye in the crem. She was necking with her boyfriend Barry at the time.

'Fucking bone sherbet,' Barry had said, wrestling her on to the lime-green terrazzo in the remembrance garden. 'Dead people's DNA joins with ewer DNA. Nasty business.'

Barry was a trainee incinerator in the crem. His main job was to clean out the crematory.

'Bone salts will burn a hole in your eyeball!'

Squinting, she was just about able to see it: a blurry outgrowth, stuck to her eyeball.

'Bullshit!' she'd screamed. 'Get it out!'

By the time they'd finished tussling on the ground, kissing, and then laughing, the grit was gone. Dropping the last of mamgu's candy stripe bedsheets, blood-stained from coughing fits, into the basket, Rachel wishes she'd let him go further.

'Tried Vanish and everything,' says Fay. 'Won't come out.'

They carry the baskets towards the door, wind splaying the mops of hydrangea bushes. Fay pops her head into the dining room.

'I'm off to get your prescription mam,' she says.' Won't be long.'

Rachel hangs around in the hallway, eager to return to her bedroom, to the striptease. By the time her mother has finished queuing at the chemist, and collected her brother Rhidian from football practice, she'll have been gone for an hour at least.

'Make sure you make her another cuppa, Rach,' says Fay.

Back in her bedroom, with her mother out on errands, Rachel changes into a different bra. A jewel-green balcony bra, with lace sides and a multi-way strap system: a birthday present from Barry. Adjusting the hook and eye setting so that the bra fits tightly around her body, accentuating her bosoms, Rachel remembers the day Barry bought her the bra.

At first he wouldn't come into the shop. He was scared of the hot pink window lights, the mannequins in complicated lingerie, the chandeliered matt-black rooms extending backwards like some impenetrable cave system.

'Where the fuck are their heads?' he said, gesturing at the mannequins.

'There's a sale on,' she said. 'Hurry up.'

He'd followed her around the showrooms like a dog, checking his phone all the while. The shop, a new Victoria's Secrets outlet, made Rachel feel as if she was somewhere more exciting than the geriatric shopping centre she visited every other Saturday with her mother: the glow of chandeliers dissolved her worries; the sugared, marshmallowy scent of body mists and pillow sprays made her forget about the funk of dust and Covona cough syrup in the house; the brittle light in her bedroom; the endless funeral corteges. After she'd selected the bra, Barry carried it to the back of the shop, handling it as though it were a grenade.

'Broad we burned yesterday had implants,' he said, when they shared a can of Monster in the food plaza afterwards. 'Tits went fuckin snap crackle pop.'

'Tits don't explode, dickhead,' she said, laughing, but also not laughing.

'Col nearly had a heart attack, pussy.'

Colin was a skinny twenty-five-year-old white guy with cornrows, who was also Barry's supervisor on the training scheme.

'We had to wipe this jizzy goo off the glass.'

A black Volvo turns in from the carriageway, crawling slowly towards the cemetery at the top of the cul de sac, metallic coachwork flinging shapes into the sky. Only a few days after hearing Barry's story, Rachel found herself undressing in the window. It had happened accidentally at first, whilst she was changing from nightwear into her day clothes. A hearse driver glanced towards her window, his eyes tarrying for longer than they should have on the creamy undulating sweep of skin across her chest, the peaks of her breasts. It was a look that confirmed something Rachel had only ever known theoretically beforehand: that she was real, and fully alive. When she saw the hearse stall before the gates, then start again, the driver's foot uneven on the gas, she knew then that she'd stolen something from death, a moment in time that should have belonged to death, and death alone. As if her life force was so pure, so compelling, so potent, it had the power to transfix, to stop time, to hold death at bay.

Rachel steps closer to the windowpane, willing this new driver to turn around. On the casket in the back of the vehicle, an elaborate arrangement of aster, myrtle, and wax flowers, spells out NAN. With a draught from the window frame quickening against the skin of her torso as she works the final hook loose, Rachel drops the bra to her feet.

Afterwards she takes a tray of tea and biscuits into mamgu in the dining room. Manoeuvring her right hand so that it supports the weight of the tray, she uses her left hand to twist the doorknob anti-clockwise, feeling her way towards a bedside table wedged between the wall and headboard of mamgu's bed. Throughout the striptease in the window, the driver's gaze had remained fixed on the cemetery gates, the white pipe of the smokestack beyond, somehow she hadn't managed to divert his attention, but afterwards in spite of the setback, the anti-climax, Rachel feels the same sense of having triumphed.

'You should open the curtains mamgu. It's pitch black, you need Vitamin D.'

Rachel tugs the pull cord of the curtains. Violet lifts herself into a sitting position, an ingot of light from a gap in the curtains skimming across the surface of her hair.

'You shouldn't be in here. Full of germs. Girl your age should be out enjoying herself!'

When Rachel was little, it was mamgu who defended her right to play in the garden during funerals, whereas her mother insisted she play with dolls in her room. According to great auntie Meryl, mamgu was also the first woman in the village to ride a bike and to wear trousers: high-waisted ivory bell bottoms made from cast-off silk parachute panels from the munitions factory. Rachel wonders what she'd make of the strip.

'I'm going out in a bit,' she says. 'Won't be long.'

'Take your time,' says mamgu.

Rachel arrives at the cemetery minutes later. Barry is at the rear entrance of the crematorium, leaning on the hoe he uses to pick out bone fragments, wedding rings, pacemakers.

'Left my pasty in the burns unit,' he says. 'Back in a mo.'

As he disappears into the belly of the building, Rachel imagines him being sucked up the smokestack like a pinball.

'Forgot to kiss one of the corpsicles goodbye, is it?' she says, when he returns.

Barry chomps down on his pasty.

'Nah. Dead love is more Colin's style. Or, as we say in the business, cracking open a cold one.'

'Minging,' she says.

They walk towards the copse outside the west gate, where the bluebells reach up higher than their calves.

'Shoulda seen the one we fried yesterday,' he says. 'Fifteen she was. Got lost up some mountain. Rescuer stripped her clothes off, then and there. Had to lie down bollock-naked right next to her. Warm her up. Course, it was too late. Anyway, we fire her up when fuck me, she bounces up like a bloody jack in the box!'

'You told me before,' she says. 'You said she was eighteen, not fifteen.'

Barry's lips are dry, his mouth no wider than his nose, his tongue wedged like ham into the gap between his front teeth. He shakes his head like he's shaking out thoughts.

'Nah. You're thinking of that student from the pile-up over Neath way. Tilted his head towards the glass half-way through. Fuck me. Glowing like a Belisha beacon it was. Didn't burn like fucking normal skulls.'

'I got something to tell you too,' she says, interrupting.

For weeks now, Rachel has been wanting to tell Barry about the striptease. For one thing, she wants to prove to him that she's no longer scared of bone sherbet, or worm food, or the DNA of dead people, or any of the other creepy-ass things he always brags about. But no sooner has she started speaking than a cracking sound surfaces beyond the copse.

'What the hell was that?' she says.

Barry looks in the direction of the disturbance, burping in a leisurely fashion.

'Can't see nuthin. Praps it's dead fuckers.'

A gigantic shape has appeared on the boundary of the field Barratts recently bought to build new houses; for a second it looks like a horse. A second shape, browny-black, materialises alongside the first shape, this time at the end of the path, where a small kissing gate separates the copse from the field.

'Ha. Dave the warden's dogs,' laughs Barry. 'Proper bastards. Know the bony bits left in the ash after a burning? Gobble them up like doggie biscuits! Fuckin psychos!'

A Siberian husky and an Alsatian, ears forward, tails wagging stiffly, are staring through the beech trees into the copse. Rachel hears one of them whine: an anxious uncertain kind of sound.

'Worse than brain eating zombie dogs,' says Barry.

The Alsatian trots slowly down the path, his body arced outwards to the side, paws suspended in the air between each step. Behind him the husky barks. Terrified, Rachel runs in the direction of the cemetery, the dogs loping after her through the bluebells.

'Ewe'll just excite em even more,' yells Barry.

Beside the entrance gate, Rachel dives into an old sprawling hawthorn hedge. The dogs have closed in on her within seconds, burying their snouts in the foliage, sniffing and snorting and barking.

Barry reaches the edge of the hedge: his knobbly legs framed by leaves.

'Al. Elvis. C'mon boys,' she hears him say.

The dogs are undaunted, immovable. Rachel pushes backwards into the hedge, her hands splayed behind her to guide her. In the fretwork of leaves she feels safer, reduced to a blurry patchwork of flesh and dark fabrics, indeterminate, unreal: a protective mist of 'Aqua Kiss' body spray keeping her actual scent from the dogs. Scooching back further and further, something licks dryly against her hand, against the bony bump on the inside of her wrist.

Nettles.

Footsteps smack the pathway on the other side of the hedge.

'Al. Elvis!' says a second, older voice. 'Come away from there!'

The dogs bark furiously, recognizing their owner Dave's voice. Reluctantly they pull away from the hedge. With her wrist burning up like a motherfucker, Rachel waits for the throbbing in her body to subside, for the hedge to stop beating in sync. When she emerges, Barry is perched on a crumbling headstone outside the folly where Dave lives, smirking.

'What the hell are you laughing at?' she says. 'Mam says they can turn in the heat. Auntie Audrey's dog Bandit went apeshit, tore her mouth off. Had to keep her lip in the freezer til the ambulance came.'

'Shouldna been snogging him then, dirty skank!' says Barry, laughing.

'You're such a twat sometimes,' she says, sauntering away from him, nursing her wrist.

He catches up with her a few yards from the gate.

'You don't want your mum seeing that!' he says, eyeing the nettle rash. 'Looks like syph.'

The rash looks even worse than before: puffed-out circular white welts that remind Rachel of Barry's bullshit stories about popping skin, and exploding tits, and leftover corpse goo.

'I'll get you dock leaves,' says Barry.

Fay is standing in the kitchen, her face frozen with fury, when Rachel arrives home twenty minutes later. The fluorescent tube fixed to the ceiling tiles whirrs and flickers like some living organism, making the light unpredictable.

'I went for a walk,' says Rachel. 'I haven't done anything wrong.'

Fay fills the kettle to the max line, the rush of water reverberating in Rachel's stomach. In the whirling steam of boiling water, it occurs to Rachel that perhaps she and her mother are doomed to collide with each other for eternity: anti-particles, isotopes of identical elements.

'Huh. A walk. Think I was born yesterday?'

After the incident with the dogs, Rachel had followed Barry to their favourite spot inside the cemetery: a secret place behind the junction box in the remembrance garden. Barry shuffled through the dock leaves in his lap, as if he'd lost his place in a book, all the while picking at his fingernail. Leaning over, she'd plucked a leaf from his lap, applying it to the underside of her wrist. Working the sap into her skin, she felt his outbreaths hovering over her arm, like molecular clouds, stellar nurseries, with a denseness at their core that suddenly thrilled her. 'Your turn,' she said, handing the leaf back. As he rubbed, something moved through her body, first in small ghostly waves, then with greater frequency: a larger version of the energy she felt during the striptease, as though she were displaced, diffuse, outside time—hooked into something greater than herself. Guiding his hand up her arm, across the ridge of her clavicle, she pulled him towards the narrow gully between her skin and the underwiring of her bra. But then he'd pulled away from her breast, muttering something about 'frying time'. Behind the cypress trees separating the remembrance garden from the avenue, she heard the locust drone of another funeral cortege.

'Don't go,' she'd said, 'Please.' But he had.

Fay hands Rachel the tea tray, forcing her to uncross her arms.

'I gave her a cuppa already. Three fig rolls and a garibaldi. Ask her yourself.'

The tingling in Rachel's breasts is like infrasound, making her feel exposed and ashamed but also queasy. Suddenly she pictures hacking her tits off to kill the noise, presenting them to her mother on the tea tray, like John the Baptist's head. *Here you fucking go. Hope you're satisfied.*

'All that sugar will be the end of her,' says Fay.

Rachel takes the tea into her mamgu. The clutter seems craggier than earlier, impassable, as if somebody sneaked in extra boxes in the meantime. Back in the spring, when she and her mother carried a Z-bed and heater into the dining room overlooking the front garden, Rachel was excited about the move. It would be fun to have another adult in the house. To celebrate, Barry had fished out a bouquet of leftover amaranths from the front steps of the crematorium. 'Moving in present for your gran' he'd said, ripping the tag off. But as the days passed, and the coughing escalated, a kind of panic had taken root in Rachel's stomach: panic but also anger and defiance. It was a weird, garish mash-up of inappropriate emotions that made Rachel want to tell mamgu to shut the fuck up every time she coughed, even though she loved her more than anyone.

'Wake up,' she says. 'I got you another cuppa.'

Rachel plants a kiss on mamgu's forehead, avoiding the spidery mole above her nose.

'Tea'll go cold. Please wake up.'

But mamgu's skin is too soft and too hard all at once; generating an aftershock that tingles beneath the surface of Rachel's lips like frostnip. When she still doesn't move after a second kiss, Rachel suddenly remembers Barry's story about the girl on the mountain and the rescuer. *Mountain rescuer had to strip her clothes off then and there, lie down bollock-naked next to her, warm her up like.*

Idiot. And yet.

Rachel strips down to her underwear, the same jewel-green balcony bra, pressing herself into her grandmother, closing the gap between their bodies. But the barrier between them is impenetrable, and like a flitting fly, or an oppositely charged particle, Rachel knows that she can only ever hover over her mamgu's dead body, never quite landing or connecting. Seconds pass, but nothing happens, except for the dull thud of something falling behind the heater: soot from the chimney maybe, or a bluebird chick. A weird sound escapes the core of Rachel's body, nothing like her regular voice.

'Thought I heard something?' says Fay, appearing in the doorway.

Fay's eyes flit across Rachel and Violet, as if she's sifting through shadows.

'What are you doing? What the hell is wrong with you?'

The last cortege of the day is already approaching the wings of the cul-de-sac by the time Rachel reaches her bedroom. Shoving a chair against the door, she whacks the volume on her air-pods into the red.

'Doctor Streeter's on her way,' says Fay, banging on the door, her voice ghostly, remote, through the music.

A VW turns into the cul-de-sac: a two-toned silver camper van with glistening chrome trim, a teal blue surfboard trailing greenery and flowers from the luggage rack, and a pale plywood coffin framed by a split screen of small bus-like side windows.

'Be down in a minute,' says Rachel. 'Promise.'

Rachel steps into the bay, into a slant of dusty, late afternoon light. Already she knows that it's over: the striptease changes nothing, saves nobody. In exposing her flesh to the mourners, perhaps all she's really doing is revealing something of her own shared mortality; in that sense it was more like a confession. And yet, as a fleet of three white stretch Beetles follow the silver camper van up the road, and a mourner shoots a baffled, backward glance towards her window, Rachel remembers something Barry said. Some people didn't give up without a fight, he said. They pulled their arms up to their chest like they were boxing, balled their hands up into tight angry fists. Sometimes they even sucker-punched the furnace window, poor fuckers. For the final time, with tears streaming down her face, Rachel slowly, defiantly, unhooks her bra.

asgard

Eleanor walks the dog along the gravel track towards the Skirrid.

'Go!' she says, as they arrive at the stile. 'Go on!'

The dog's ears stiffen. He cocks his head to the side. Sheets of cloud obliterate the pathway to the summit but judging by the volume of vehicles in the car park, Eleanor guesses a few hikers remain on the ridge. When the dog doesn't move and merely stares, Eleanor considers tying him to the stile at the top of the track where he might be seen.

'What are you waiting for?!' she says. 'Go!'

Eleanor throws a ball into the woods beyond the stile.

'Go! I'll be fine.'

The dog dives under the stile, chasing the ball into the woods. Eleanor makes a dash for her car. Manoeuvring out of the car park into the dual carriageway, she half expects to see him sprinting after her down the track, his soft tongue blowing backwards like a scarf, but the rear-view mirror reveals a deserted trail, snaking into the woods at a queer angle. Steadying her hands on the wheel, Eleanor turns into the carriageway and drives away.

Eleanor had acquired the dog at Cardiff Dogs Home six months earlier. A young man who dealt with her application said they were the 'perfect match': a description that pleased Eleanor so much she repeated it to Joyce, an acquaintance from the carers' group in the village.

'It's too soon,' Joyce said. 'You need time.'

Eleanor's mother Sybil had died three weeks earlier. Complications arising from pneumonia and sepsis.

'Go on a cruise. You've been running around after other people for god knows how long. A dog will run you ragged.'

'I'm not a child Joyce. I know what I'm doing.'

At first the relationship worked well. The dog was something new in Eleanor's life. By immersing herself in the challenges of her new routine, she imagined that she could become a new person. But as the weeks went by, and then months, whilst the increased house chores and daily walks proved tiring, the clearing of dog excrement dispiriting, what Eleanor found the most difficult was how the dog always followed her like a shadow. Always waiting, always wanting, always there. The familiar whimpering outside the cloakroom when she needed the toilet, the watching eyes from behind the French doors when she hung out laundry, and worst of all, the weight of the dog's body on the arch of her foot as she tried to watch television, heightening her awareness of a sickly low-voltage restlessness, flickering through the circuits of her mind.

'What's wrong with you?' she'd yell. 'Why can't you leave me alone?'

It was a restlessness with which Eleanor was familiar. A few weeks before Sybil died, Eleanor had found herself parked on a stretch of gleaming tarmac in the new Bay View Heights housing development on the other side of the village, with no memory of having driven there.

In the development site office, a handsome sales consultant had taken her to view the new Horizon 0.1 show home. Following him into a vast open-plan kitchen diner, Eleanor wanted to spread her limbs out on the tiles, let the cool of the marble soak in.

'On a good day, you can see all the way across the Channel,' he said.

When she returned home, her mother was crumpled on the hallway floor.

'I was going to phone the police—I tripped on the runner again—it's a nuisance. Where were you all morning?'

Eleanor felt sick with fresh guilt. She'd only gone to collect her mother's medication, a journey that should have taken twenty minutes. But it was the day of the village raft race, traffic was heavier than usual, and Eleanor had opted for the back roads, a route that must have taken her past the development.

'Traffic was murder. Sorry mum.'

'I can't bear to think of you—out there—alone. If it weren't for me—you'd have no one.'

Eleanor helped her mother to her feet. For the remainder of the day, whilst removing a number of trip hazards from the hallway and living room, including a pretty rug made in the Atlas Mountains she and a boyfriend haggled over in a souk in Marrakech, Eleanor scrutinized her mother's words. Maybe there *was* nothing out there. Maybe there *was* no one. Maybe she was, all alone. Steeling herself against a squall of wind that caught her off-guard as she opened the front door, she dragged the rug and some side tables into the garage.

Eleanor tried hard to find common ground with other dog owners. One day, as she was walking the dog across the village recreation ground, a community councillor called Wendy sidled up to her, launching into an unsolicited rant about the cost of boarding kennels and veterinary surgeons, offering details about her labradoodle's chronic psoriasis. Relief surged through Eleanor's body. She wanted to reach out and touch Wendy's wrist.

'Oh, they're such a tie, aren't they?' she said, blushing.

Wendy's eyes probed Eleanor's body like infrared. Turning away, she called her dog Kenny to heel.

'I'm not sure what you mean,' she said, finally.

'Oh, nothing really,' said Eleanor. 'Obviously I'd never be without him.'

The morning afterwards, as if her comments were in some way to blame, Eleanor awoke to discover the dog had shit blood on the memory foam dog bed. She phoned the emergency vet line.

'He's fat,' said the vet during the check-up. 'You should walk him more. How long do you walk him for?'

The vet was a distant cousin from the more aspirational wing of Eleanor's family, which now included a new mayor in the States, a doctor in New Zealand, and a hedge fund manager. Meanwhile, Eleanor had always been a disappointment to her own mother, having worked most of her life as a part-time clerical assistant at the job centre.

'What about the blood?' Eleanor said, ignoring the question, feeling a sudden need to be firm. 'It was all over the bed.'

'Standing water,' said the vet. 'Don't let him drink from it.'

Eleanor increased the length of her dog walks from one to two hours. She purchased a Fitbit in the Debenhams sale. Whenever she stopped to examine her progress, her heart rate, the number of steps taken, the dog reproached her with a silent stare. Unable to distract herself properly with technology, Eleanor travelled further afield in search of variety, her peace of mind now contingent not only upon her ability to placate the dog, but also by a growing need to distract herself from the abstract yearning for something at the core of her, a yearning that intensified daily.

One weekend, she took the dog up the Skirrid, a mountain thirty miles to the east, which was the furthest they'd ever been together. She liked the word 'Skirrid,' the rattle bag of consonants from the old Welsh word 'ysgyryd,' meaning shattered or split. It pleased her to say it out loud, as if she was articulating something important, something relevant.

The dog ran ahead of her as soon as they arrived in the car park, bounding up the gravel pathway that led to the summit. She saw him slip under a stile, disappear into woodland. At first Eleanor didn't hurry; the dog would be waiting by the trees. When she reached the gate on the other side of the woodland however, and the dog was still nowhere to be seen, Eleanor increased her pace. Finally, at the trig point, she saw his tail poking out from behind an outcrop.

'Don't run away again! What were you thinking?'

The dog's eyes shone with a complex lustre that was unfamiliar to Eleanor. Where had he been for the last hour? What had he seen? As they clambered down the path towards the woods, a yellow-eyed brindle dog without a collar emerged suddenly from behind a waymarking post. Eleanor remembered an article she'd read about strays in Chernobyl: pet dogs who escaped the disaster, who lived in the forests with wolves. This brindle dog was a stray, she was sure. Eleanor pictured him sprinting into the wilderness beyond the Skirrid: her own dog panting in pursuit. By the time they reached the woodland at the foot of the mountain, the brindle dog had disappeared into the woods. Eleanor tightened the lead on her dog.

'Come on! It's getting late!'

It was dark by the time they arrived home. Eleanor hadn't been out this late since her days as a student in Bristol. Treating the dog to a cheese string and a stick of pepperoni, she let him climb on the sofa un-scolded. In spite of everything, it troubled her to think he might have run away from her. When she woke, having fallen asleep during the ten o' clock news, Joyce from the carers group was standing at the foot of the sofa.

'Bloody door was wide open!'

'Joyce!' she said. 'What the hell?'

Eleanor wondered for a moment whether Joyce was one of those night hags you saw when you were awake but couldn't move your body? Scanning the living room, she found that the configuration of the room no longer made sense. Why was the window to her left? Why was the door straight ahead?

'It's the middle of the night, Joyce,' she said.

Eleanor tried to lift her head from the sofa cushion, which she now realised wasn't a sofa cushion but a bolster: the bolster that came with the dog bed. She was lying on the dog bed, in the alcove, with her legs arched over the dog's sleeping body. How had she ended up here?

'The dog had a nightmare,' she said, panicking. 'I was comforting him.'

She needn't have bothered with the lie. Joyce, who she hadn't heard from in weeks, was staring into the middle-distance, wearing purple gardening clogs and her husband Terry's three-piece suit. Eleanor remembered one of the neighbours saying she'd been spotted wandering the streets at strange hours.

'Sybil here?' Joyce asked. 'Where's Sybil?'

The dog shook off layers of sleep. Hairs drifted in and out of Eleanor's line of sight like the floaters forever trapped in her eyeballs. Brushing dog hair from her jumper, she picked at a snippet of bark stuck to her forearm like a scab.

'She died, Joyce. Sybil died.'

'Christ on a bike,' said Joyce, fiddling with a button on Terry's three-piece suit. 'Bloody clothes don't fit me anymore. I look like a bin bag.'

'Pneumonia and then the sepsis kicked in. She died a few months ago.'

Joyce's hand settled on the button, becoming still. She scanned Eleanor's face without understanding, like she was reading a QR code.

'Oh, it's you Eleanor,' she said. 'You're on the floor. Does your mum know?'

'You'd better go now,' said Eleanor.

Eleanor couldn't bring herself to get up from the dog bed to see Joyce out. To get up from the dog bed would be an acknowledgment that something was wrong, that in some way she was even madder than Joyce, who drifted down the hallway trailing a dank, fruity odour.

'Cold as snowman's piss out,' she said.

After she had gone, Eleanor sat on the dog bed for hours, immobilized not only by shame, but by a clawing panic in the pit of her chest. What would people think of her? Sleeping on the dog bed. When she was a kid, nine or ten, she used to sleepwalk. A neighbour found her asleep in a bus stop in her Sooty and Sweep pyjamas. Maybe she had sleepwalked to the dog bed, anxious after the day's near loss.

When it was too cold to stay still any longer, Eleanor pulled herself up from the dog bed and made her way to the kitchen. Reaching for one of her mother's bone-china teacups from the dresser, she made herself a strong black tea. But no sooner had she touched the handle of the teacup than she began to cry. The suddenness of it took her by surprise, the crest of each crying jag hitting her like a wave, sucking everything from her body, leaving her wrung out over the kitchen sink, her face a hot puffy mess.

The dog trotted into the kitchen to stare.

'Bed,' she said. 'Go to bed.'

Following his example, she climbed upstairs. By the time she reached her bedroom, a tide of weak morning light was edging across both walls towards her bed. But to her surprise she felt lighter than usual, as if she'd cried something out of her. It was only the second time she'd cried since the death, the first time being three days after the funeral, when unable to find her Fiesta in the supermarket car park, she'd searched the parking bays until dark, a bag of frozen peas thawing wetly against her knee through the carrier.

Succumbing to sleep, she dreamed for the first time in a long time. In the dream she was spinning through space, clutching a rope light that was actually the dog's tail. It was cold but the view was to die for.

The following morning, Eleanor cleaned the house. Having completed her chores, she took a shower, examining herself in the bathroom mirror afterwards. At fifty-seven she was no longer conventionally beautiful, but there *was* something there: a residual glow. Something ignited inside her, flaring outwards hopefully for a second. Dragging the Moroccan rug back into the house, she repositioned it in the sitting room in front of the French doors. The fringe was grubby, a little grey: nothing the rug cleaner couldn't tackle. As she separated the stuck-together tassels, the dog appeared in the patio window.

'What is it boy?' she asked.

The dog jumped up against the window, leaving paw marks on the glass, a trail of careening slobber. He barked impatiently, angrily. She hadn't taken him out for his walk yet. Letting him in through the patio doors, she noticed something about his eyes. The lenses looked cloudier, emulsified, having lost their mountain lustre.

'What is it?' she said. 'What do you want?'

Driving northwest for the coast now, the bitten-off flank of the Skirrid flashes behind Eleanor as she turns off the A465 to join the A49. After letting the dog in through the patio doors the previous day, it had become clear to Eleanor that just as she needed to free herself from the life that had defined her thus far, she also needed to free the dog.

'I'll take you back,' she'd said. 'I'll take you to the Skirrid.'

Pulling into a service station to buy coffee, she pictures him nosing around the waymarking post with the brindle dog, bedding down into cosy warm earth, all the while pushing aside the fear that he could freeze or else starve on the mountain. No, if the worst came to the worst, some hikers would find him in the woods.

But as she removes her gloves to drink the coffee, a stiff white hair protruding from her middle knuckle catches her attention. Last week she yanked a similar specimen from her groin. Gripping the base of the hair with her tweezers, Eleanor rips it out quickly from the root. Immediately, a hot searing pain fans across the back of her hand, a pain that is disproportionate, disorienting.

Eleanor sips the coffee to distract herself.

But it's too late.

Blood springs to the surface of her knuckle.

A fortnight after Sybil's fall in the hallway, as they'd taken a late breakfast of scrambled eggs in the living room, a bubble of dark gritty blood with the texture of spent coffee beans had similarly surfaced in the corner of Sybil's mouth. Within hours, Sybil had been transferred from Accident & Emergency to the ICU with suspected sepsis. Eleanor stayed at her mother's bedside for a day and a night and then another day, not moving, not eating, barely breathing. The high-impact antibiotics weren't working. Sybil was on a ventilator. A tangle of limp catheters and feeding tubes and IV lines on the bed mapped out a kind of slow unravelling in Eleanor's mind.

The fall was her fault.

Eleanor visited the ward toilets in a daze. Although she hadn't eaten for days, she was badly constipated. In a toilet dedicated to patients, she took a shit. It was the only shit she'd ever taken in a public place. Afterwards, she couldn't go back to the ward. She had nothing left to give or say. Leaving the hospital right away, she bought a coke and a magazine about decorating from the WRVS kiosk in the lobby and went home. Her mother died an hour later, never recovering consciousness; the medics never asked Eleanor why she vanished. If they had, Eleanor would have said she was distressed and exhausted. But it wasn't that.

Eleanor pulls on her gloves. The truth was she was terrified. Terrified of being blindsided by events, of being swamped by what might be, what would be; terrified of the groundswell of her emotions, pulling her backwards towards some dark singularity. This was why she'd abandoned her mother. This was why she'd abandoned the dog.

It was better to avoid pain at all costs. Quit while you were ahead.

And yet here she was. Sitting in a service station in the dead of night, with the same darkness closing in on her.

When she returns to the car park at the foot of the Skirrid, no vehicles remain. Anxious of what she might see in the dog's eyes, disappointment, betrayal, contempt even, Eleanor sits for a while in the car listening to the world service. There was still time to make amends, surely?

Opening the car door, Eleanor focuses the light from her smartphone on the stony pathway ahead. The pathway steepens and narrows after an unfamiliar bend, the stile rearing into view like a portal.

'Macsen. Come on Macsen!'

The woodland beyond the stile is denser than she remembers, the path through the trees a broken line now. As the darkness plummets through her body, Eleanor holds on to the crossbar of the stile.

'Macsen. I'm really sorry,' she yells.

A crackling sound snaps through Eleanor's body like a charge. Eleanor focuses her light on the line of the path, adjusting the brightness setting. Twenty yards ahead, where the path widens, is a pale ghost-like animal, a dog, the weight of its body shifted forwards, head tilted to the right.

Eleanor climbs over the stile.

'Macsen?'

The dog lifts a paw at her voice. His tail wags to the right. Slowly but then gradually faster. When he runs through the undergrowth towards her, breaking twigs without a care, the familiar eager slant of his body, the gleeful lolling of his tongue, overwhelms her, and she feels herself expanding to contain all their hopes, expanding until she is bigger than the dark.

'We're going home now,' she says.

RATTUS
RATTUS

Deb straightens up the car on the road. The next-door neighbour, Steve, is waving at her from behind a sagging chain link gate at the side of his house, jerking his arm strangely, like he might be having a stroke. When Deb takes a closer look, she realises that he isn't waving at all, but gesturing towards her house.

'Back in a second ok?' she says to Rhys, who is strapped into the car seat behind her. 'I have to find out what Steve wants.'

Steve lumbers down the side path towards Deb, rubbing at a crusty tumour on his nose.

'You've got rats,' he says. 'Plural. Jen was having coffee in the breakfast room. Thought they were squirrels. But they weren't squirrels, Christ no.'

Steve shapes his hands to indicate the size of the rats, which to Deb seems pretty small in the scheme of things.

'Came through your hedge into ours,' he says.

'I'll call someone. I'll call the landlord.'

Steve shakes his head from side to side. 'Best if I show you,' he says.

Brambles have laid siege to the flower borders, which loop and arc towards the lawn. A faded circle indicates the spot where a trampoline might have stood. Deb follows Steve towards the hedge that runs the length of her garden.

'Here,' he says, leaning over.

Surrounding the drain cover at the foot of the hedge are several fist-sized rat holes. One, two, three, four, all lined up in a bank of disturbed earth. Further over, amongst nettles and bindweed, is another hole, this one more ragged. Using a long-handled screwdriver he unveils from his overalls, Steve prods the holes one by one.

'Jen saw five, maybe six,' he says. 'She was having coffee.'

'Six? I thought you said four?' says Deb.

'There were a couple in the shrubs. The others were playing on the bird feeder, bold as brass.'

Deb finds herself fixating on the word 'playing'. The idea of killing something capable of playing makes her anxious, uneasy.

'I have to go check on Rhys,' she says. 'I left him in the car.'

'You have to get rid of them, Deborah,' says Steve, using her full name, for effect. 'We can't have rats.'

Deb remembers the story about an Olympic rower who died when rat piss infected the blisters on his palm; the rugby player who fell ill after drinking from a beer bottle contaminated by rat's urine, in a pub cellar. Somehow, the stories aren't enough to neutralise the power of the word 'playing'. The rats were juveniles, babies. Playing on a bird table in the sunshine.

'Of course, Steve,' she says. 'Course I will.'

Deb googles 'humane rat control' from her desktop. Her search returns a site promoting homemade citrus sprays, complicated instructions on Wikihow for making humane rat traps using oil drums and peanut butter, a thread on the benefits of pouring soiled cat litter down rat holes.

Deb would love to get a cat, or a dog, but the tenants contract forbids it.

Deb face-times Greg from her phone.

'We've got rats,' she says. 'Steve's being a total asshole.'

Deb's husband Greg works five thousand miles away as a diver on an offshore oil rig in the Gulf of Mexico, repairing rig anchors at the bottom of the ocean. Greg's image freezes during their conversation, as though he's there, but not there.

'It's five in the morning,' says Greg, after a longer glitch than usual. 'You woke me up.'

'We'll talk later, sorry,' says Deb.

Deb has almost finished putting Rhys to bed when Steve rings the doorbell.

'About the rats. When were you thinking of phoning the landlord?'

'Not sure yet,' she says.

'All he'll do is phone the council, they're bloody useless.'

Rhys, who has attached himself like a burr to Deb's legs is studying a gleaming scar that circumnavigates Steve's head.

'You want to make sure he's safe, don't you?' says Steve, pointing at Rhys. 'Council don't even check the drains. Down Lamby Way, they've got a retarded guy with a dead falcon on a string. Swings the falcon round all day to scare the rats. Bloody joke.'

'Maybe they're being environmentally friendly,' says Deb.

Steve screws his features up small.

'Back in the day they had rat pits. Brought in terriers, tore the bastards to pieces. Not that I condone blood sports or animal cruelty, but, well—'

'No, of course not,' says Deb.

Steve peers over Deb's shoulder into the hallway as though he thinks she might be hiding more rats in the house.

'Would you like a cup of tea?' she says. 'I'm putting Rhys to bed.'

'No, that's quite alright,' says Steve, forming a stop sign with his hand. 'I'll get you the number of a private company.'

When Steve has gone, Deb takes a Nurofen to relieve her headache, which is gathering behind her eyes like a storm surge. Maybe she could block the air grille in the kitchen? The vent hose from the tumble dryer? Perhaps, if she managed to lock down all the entry and exit points, she wouldn't need to contact anybody.

Later, when she checks in on Rhys, she finds him coiled around the banister post on the upstairs landing, a line of dinosaur figures arranged like watchmen against the stair riser.

'Why is Mr Henderson scared of rats?' he says, as she tucks him back into bed.

'He's not scared. He just hates them.'

'Did the rats make the line in his head?'

Deb plants a kiss on Rhys's forehead, which is clammy and whiter than the pillow.

'Tomorrow we're going to the play centre,' she says, by way of an answer. 'Go to sleep.'

Deb contacts a local rat catcher with five-star reviews who arrives promptly the following morning.

'If the babies are in the garden, the colony has become emboldened,' he says.

Deb can't get past the words 'babies' and 'garden'. The rat catcher's holdall is gaping open like a hungry mouth on the path. Inside are several Tupperware boxes.

'I read traps are more humane. I read—'

Deb cannot muster up the necessary conviction in her voice. She fears looking like a snowflake in front of the rat catcher, who, with his ponytail and silver skull rings, looks like he might be into death metal.

'End of the day, do what works,' she says, losing confidence.

The rat catcher scoops lilac oats from the Tupperware boxes into a series of see-through plastic bags. Having spent the previous evening reading about rodenticides, Deb knows that after gorging on poison, the rat pups will curl into small pulsing balls and bleed out.

'Went to another lady's house a couple of weeks ago. Animal lover. Insisted on snap traps. Besides herself she was, when I went back. Hedgehog had gotten himself stuck in the trap. Missing his front paw right down to the bone.'

Steve has appeared behind the privet hedge that separates the two properties.

'Oh, traps can be very cruel,' he says, with a kind of glee. 'Extremely cruel. Only a small chance of connecting with the skull.'

The rat catcher swivels half-way towards Steve, whose face is framed by a small ragged gap in the hedge. Steve extends his hand through the gap.

'Steve,' he says. 'Steve Henderson. They were on my bird feeder, bold as you like.'

The rat catcher seems irritated by the neighbour. A squint in his left eye means that Deb can't be sure where he's looking, or at whom.

'Baiting's the only solution here,' he says.

'As I thought,' says Steve.

The rat catcher places bait in the holes. Earth rises up like quicksand over the grey bony mass in his wrist.

'I'll check the perimeter for any other signs of them,' he says, rising to his feet. 'Looks like you've got a few exposed areas.'

'Any chance you can take a quick look in ours?' says Steve, interrupting.

The rat catcher feeds a black and red business card through the hedge.

'Best if you make an appointment mate,' he says.

Deb makes a coffee for the ratcatcher. Was it two scoops of sugar or three? White or black? Why was she always so distracted? So preoccupied. The rat catcher ransacks the shed at the back of the garden, pulling out a body board, a play tent, a selection of rotting brightly-coloured plastic items, creating the impression that the shed is bigger inside than out.

'I baited the shed,' he says, appearing in Deb's kitchen doorway, minutes later. 'Reeked like cat piss.'

Deb hands the rat catcher his coffee, wondering about the poison on his hands.

'You got to know how it connects,' he says, scanning the kitchen. 'Sewers, drains, vents, cavities.'

Deb imagines a stinking labyrinth of dark scuttling beasts beneath the house.

Rats with baby faces.

Half-alive, half-dead, crawling.

How far down did it go?

'Single pair produces fifteen thousand offspring a year,' says the rat catcher, downing the coffee, glancing over at her. 'Little bastards do it twenty times a day.'

Deb imagines the same contaminated hand that entered the rat hole, entering her.

'Oh, righty ho. Well, thanks for coming at such short notice,' she says.

Deb takes Rhys to a soft play centre near their old house. As soon as Rhys is in the play castle, she phones Greg.

'Rat catcher came. Reckons there are loads of them. A colony.'

'We live in the countryside, Deborah,' says Greg, in a vaguely condescending tone. 'There are rats everywhere.'

'So I'm supposed to let them fuck about all day and night until they piss in Rhys's paddling pool? Until he gets Weil's disease?'

'I didn't say that. Calm down.'

The phrase 'calm down' makes Deb's blood boil. She imagines Greg lying dead at the bottom of the ocean with a rig anchor bisecting his body.

'Try and be more supportive then,' she says. 'I've got to go.'

Rhys runs over from the pirate ship as soon as Deb hangs up. A random child comes to sit at their table, sucking on a lollipop, scratching. Deb wonders if she could love another person as much as Rhys.

'Slide,' says Rhys. 'I want to go on the slide.'

The slide is a huge double-drop plastic tube accessed from the uppermost level of the play centre. A few years back, somebody stuck a blade to the inside of the tube with chewing gum.

'We've got to go home,' she says. 'Next time.'

That night she goes early to bed, letting Rhys fall asleep at her side. Watching the rise and fall of his scrawny six-year-old ribcage, his hair spread out damply across his cheek, the scab on his knee like a jewel, Deb knows that killing the rats is the right thing to do. Her duty as a parent, in fact.

But at three, a chill blue light bleeds through the curtain crack, waking her.

The house security light.

Pulling the weighted duvet over both of them, Deb pictures a tide of angry vengeful rats rising up the drainpipes, gnawing at the security light cables, tripping the electrics. But no, that was stupid. It must have been a bat, or a moth, she thinks. Migrating sparrows even. All she had to do was dial down the sensitivity on the security light and she'd be back in bed in no time.

When she reaches the garden, the night is much colder than she imagined. In the levelling LED glare of the security light, the garden has the insubstantial two-dimensional quality of a film set. She could push the shed over with her finger.

Tightening the toggle on her hood, Deb flips over a mop bucket to reach the light.

She twists the dial but nothing happens. She tries again but still nothing.

Making her way back down the garden path towards the house and the breaker unit on the first-floor landing, she finds the back door shut tight. Something scuttles behind her. Shoving the door with her hand and then, with her ass, the horror of her situation finally registers. She has locked herself out of the house.

'Deborah? That you?' says a man's voice.

Deb continues to push against the sash bar with the heels of her hands, having worked her fingers into a gap beneath the window frame to heave the sash up. She remembers the story about a breastfeeding mother who woke to find a rat on her pillow, drawn in by the odour of sour milk.

'Deborah?' says the voice again, louder.

Looking over, and upwards, she sees Steve, leaning so far out of his bedroom window a tiny push could tip him out.

'I'm ok Steve. I'm going in now,' she says, lying.

'No. I'm coming over. Wait there.'

When Deb unbolts the side gate, Steve is dressed in day clothes: a camo jacket, matching trucker hat. His cologne has a clinical after-smell.

'Rats must have triggered the security light,' he says, holding a fifty-inch rifle.

'Vintage Winchester. My father's,' he says, seeing her stare. 'The gun that won the West!'

'It's under control, Steve,' she says, hurrying after him towards the hedge. 'The rat catcher put bait down. I was going inside when you called.'

'They're everywhere you look, love,' says Steve, poking at the rat holes with his Winchester, a weird look on his face. 'Super rats. Foreign mutations. Down where Jen's brother lives, Wisbech, the bastards are resistant to rat poison.'

A high-pitched chirruping is quickly followed by a second loop of chirruping from further out in the garden by the shed. Steve yanks the rifle from a hole, spinning at the same time as Deb.

Sitting in the yellow-green patch on the lawn, slurping from a Ribena carton, is a rat. A large brown adult rat. Deb is so transfixed by details: the way the rat holds the carton like treasure, pleasure rippling through its body in spasms; the pink cord of its tail in the grass, bioluminescent as a glowstick; the curled fingers, the delicate fingernails, she forgets everything else. A half-formed thought blows through her mind like tumbleweed. The garden belongs as much to the rat as to anyone.

Steve lifts his rifle, pulls the trigger. A flash of gassy light from the muzzle illuminates a flicker in the rat's eyes. A small squalid shrinking movement. Terror.

'Gonna need gloves, a grabber, some plastic bags,' says Steve, walking towards the hump on the lawn.

Shockwaves pulse like bile through Deb's body.

'You've got to go now, Steve. Please,' she says.

Steve turns towards her with a branch. For a second she thinks he might beat her. Poke her eyes out. Instead he shoves the branch towards her face. Impaled on the end of it is a misshapen bulge like a sock puppet, which quivers along its length and becomes still.

'Please don't shoot any more of them. I don't want you to,' she says.

Steve drops the rat at her feet.

'You have to go home now,' she says. 'This is my house.'

Steve kicks the rat a little closer.

'Your type, you haven't a fucking clue,' he says.

Deb can't be sure how long she remains rooted to the spot after he's gone, listening to the tick of her body. It isn't until the security light times out, until the garden falls dark again, that she remembers about Rhys, alone upstairs.

How could she have forgotten?

Lifting a plant pot from the windowsill, she hurls it directly at the window. Cracks streak through the glazing all at once, galvanizing her into a decision. A malevolent energy, more unsettling than the rats, had been closing in on them for god knows how long. If she stayed it would swallow them up. Upstairs, having checked on Rhys, holding her hand to his face to check his breathing, she packs an overnight case, Rhys's new spaceship Trunki, and a bag of snacks, arranging them in a line by the front door. At first light she would leave and not return.

When she checks the garden a final time, the rat is still splayed on the path, smaller and flatter than she remembered. Using the long green Marigold gloves used to scrub the loo bowl, Deb scoops the rat from the path, feeling the weight of his life in her hands, the smallness of it, the seriousness, before lowering him into the corner of a plastic bag. Securing the bag with a knot, she places him into a second bag, then a third, in a reverse of pass-the-parcel.

'I'm sorry you didn't get to finish your Ribena,' she says.

As soon as the rat is safely swaddled, she carries him away from the existing rat burrows to a neutral no-man's land at the far end of the garden. Placing him on his side in a hole, she covers him in a blanket of topsoil. Then, when the burial is complete, she uses the shimmer pen from Rhys's hobby box to write on the stem of a wooden spoon, a marker left to guard the grave, RIP RATTUS RATTUS.

SHAVING FOR DOG

Meinir slides under the surface. Through the warped lens of the bath water, the ceiling spotlights are like four alien suns, or surgical task lights in an operating theatre: their disinfecting glare cleansing her of doubt.

Emerging from the bathwater, Meinir quickly reaches for the can of shaving foam and Bic razor from the lip of the bath. There was a time, not so long ago, when the growth of fine wheat-coloured hair on her legs was exhilarating—part of a longed-for process of transformation—but the hairs are thicker now, tawnier, with a zoological quality that makes Meinir uneasy. Pressing down on the nozzle of the can, a foaming orb, the size of a golf ball, fizzes like bug spit in Meinir's hand. Working the foam onto her legs, she drags the razor against the direction of hair growth.

When she's done she steps out of the water, which is as murky and opaque as amniotic fluid. Underneath the bright zingy flesh of her legs, the hairs are still there, spring-loaded, in suspended animation, a thought that thrills Meinir even as it appals. Grafting a square of toilet tissue to a small trickling cut on her knee, she wraps a towel around her like a secret.

Back in the hotel bedroom, her mother Elena is waiting for her by a balcony window overlooking a pink-red puzzle mat of rooftops sprawling towards the Coliseum and hills. A sheer, floaty white dress makes her look more like a presence than a person: an impression reinforced by a halo of fuzzy grey hair.

'Tomorrow we'll go to the catacombs. Christians hid there to avoid persecution.'

Meinir imagines kicking her mother out of the window, seeing her shaggy sagging body spinning through space, her dress fanning outwards like wings: an urge that is nothing more than a projection of her own desire to jump, which resurfaces whenever she is at the edge of things.

Train platforms, monuments, cliffs.

'I'm going out. Look around the square,' she says, anxious to be out of the room, desperate to try out her new identity.

'Table's booked for seven,' says her mother. 'Don't be long.'

The square of toilet paper pressed to Meinir's knee detaches, twizzling downwards to the carpet like a sycamore key.

'Cut yourself to smithereens!' says Elena. 'Bloody ridiculous!'

Meinir slips down a side street off the Via Della Purificiazone, relieved to have escaped her mother, the airless claustrophobia of the hotel room. A cool breeze licks the back of her legs. With her flesh so smooth and hairless, the air is closer now: nothing separates her from the world beyond. She wonders what her boyfriend Dog would say if he could see her. A couple of days before the end of school term, as she was about to sit next to him on the school bus, he'd stretched an arm across the aisle to form a barrier.

'Rules number one, two, and three. No fucking yetis in the back!'

His laugh was a husky machine-gun rattle of ha-ha-has that punched a hole through Meinir's gut.

Hywel Williams, who was sat next to the emergency exit, rearranged a bulge in his trousers.

'Furry orgy anyone?'

Meinir knew all about shaving. It was what her friends and teachers did (though not her mother). And although she was increasingly troubled by the growth on her legs, the warm sprawling fuzz between her thighs, part of her was mesmerised by the transformation; curious about where it might lead.

'Fuck off, retard,' she said to Hywel, even though she'd known him since nursery school, even though his trousers were those pleated school trousers little boys wore.

After that she bought a whole load of shaving accessories. A bag of disposable razors with protective strips of aloe vera. A can of Gillette Venus. Accessories she'd packed in her holiday bag. Whereas at home she felt embarrassed about shaving, on holiday she could pass it off as an experiment, a one-off.

A gang of teenagers skids into the side street ahead of her, their outlines framed by the fading afternoon sun. Beyond them traffic roars, horns honk incessantly. Halfway along the street, at the corner of an alley divided by steep steps, a thin man in chinos with a ponytail yells at her from an arched doorway.

'Senorita. You got blood. You come inside. I got, how do you say, plaster?'

Glancing down quickly at her leg, Meinir sees a streak of bright watery blood careening towards her ankle from where she cut herself. Eager to get rid of the blood, she crosses the street towards the man. By the time she reaches the peeling pink building on the other side, the man is waiting for her inside the doorway, leaning against the crumbling masonry.

'Follow,' he says, gesturing to the empty courtyard behind.

A droplet of blood from Meinir's legs seeps into a stone in the courtyard, where petals from a purple bougainvillea litter the ground. She follows him into a room off the back of the courtyard, a kitchenette with blue and white ceramic floor tiles, a bike hanging from a peg on the wall. The man returns from an anteroom with a first aid kit, an oversized green suitcase with the white cross reduced to abstract markings. He rests the kit at Meinir's feet. Still troubled by the leaking of her body fluids, evidence of her former self, Meinir covers another blood spatter with her foot.

'I put it on,' he says.

Meinir nods and thanks the man with a smile, a gesture he returns by twisting his lips to the side, a sign of gas maybe, or nerves. Peeling the back off a plaster, spit forms a bubble on his lip.

'I've got to go soon,' she says.

The man applies the sticking plaster to Meinir's knee, his other hand on the exact spot on her thigh where a minute earlier, she'd felt the breeze. His flesh is as damp as a fish. Meinir knows she shouldn't have entered the courtyard, it was stupid and utterly reckless, but the truth was that none of it felt real at the time; not the fading pink sun, nor the theatrical horn honking, nor the man greeting her as Senorita. The real Meinir was still in the hotel bathroom, submerged, idling under the glare of the surgical light-head, waiting for something to happen.

'Very nice leg. Smooth like baby,' he says.

'My mother is waiting for me,' she says, or imagines she says.

The man grabs her suddenly by the wrist, his other arm already stretched over her left shoulder, blocking her exit: the sweat from his armpit a living thing, a crouching animal. He drags her down some steps to a room behind the kitchen, an empty space that stinks of bleach. A big bottle of Chicco bug spray and a pair of yellow household gloves languish on a solitary floating shelf below a window. Grabbing both her wrists now, raising her arms above her head, the man pushes her into the wall with his groin.

'I check you have more cuts ok.'

A wasp is buzzing on the window, banging its abdomen against the glass. The mere idea of a wasp would usually have Meinir flailing from one room to another in search of an escape route, but by now she can barely speak let alone move, because the man's fist is inside her, tearing through her. The pain is shocking, bewildering, but worse are the tendrils of dread, materialising like blackdamp in the newly hollowed-out voids of her body; the realisation that she can't remember anything from before this moment. As if she's been in this odd sunken room all her life, in the blank light with the bug spray and the wasp.

'No cuts but you forget to shave this part.'

His words are remote, unintelligible, on the same level as the distant traffic, the broken hum in the walls, the inert, tuneless noise of her body. The wasp vibrates as it takes off from the window, as it sways towards the man's head, first in slow motion, giddily, as if navigating a strong wind, but then faster, with greater purpose. She'd thought, mistakenly, that it was trapped behind a pane of glass. As it approaches, she sees it in detail:

the gauzy forewings, the inky eyes, a silver nimbus of hairs on its thorax, extending outwards. Years earlier she'd read something in a science book: something about the way an animal's hairs provided it with a defence mechanism, a way of sensing the vicinity of its enemies. In one picture, there was a close-up of the trigger hairs on a Venus fly trap: the lobes snapping shut around a fly. Tipitiwitchets, mamgu called them. Suddenly she can see the page in the science book; smell the colours pulsing up from the page. She remembers, too, the hairy girl in the bath, waiting to become: the accidental unbecoming moments later.

'Get off me! Fuck off!'

The man's fist becomes still in her body, like something pretending to be dead. It takes Meinir another few seconds to realise that the person yelling is none other than herself, and that her body is closing in on his fist, crunching down on the meat of his knuckles.

When she returns to the hotel room, Elena is drinking from the bottle she bought in duty free, using a plastic toothbrush cup from the bathroom.

'You left your phone here. We missed our dinner reservation.'

'I got lost. I need a shower.'

'Another ten minutes and I was going to phone the police,' she says, turning away slightly, as if she knows something happened.

Meinir retreats to the bathroom, locking the door, relocking it, her insides beating loudly, audibly. The idea of her mother finding out about the fist fuck: finding out that for the briefest of moments, her daughter was nothing more than a gaping vessel for the thin man's fist, is unbearable, humiliating. And yet it also pleases Meinir to remember the way the man had yanked his arm out of her body when she yelled; the way the wasp made him thrash the air seconds later.

'You hungry?' says Elena, through the door. 'We could still go out.'

'I'm fine. I just got lost.'

The plaster is still stuck to Meinir's knee, grimy around the edges. Meinir pictures something lurking underneath: a septic hole. But underneath there is nothing but skin, pink pristine skin, the familiar undulations of her kneecap. The shaving cut has vanished, as if it was never there. Stepping into the shower, something catches her eye: a patch of hair on the back of her thigh, a spot she must have missed earlier whilst shaving.

Elena is back on the balcony when Meinir returns to the bedroom, nursing another wine. She offers Meinir a second plastic cup from the bathroom, a half-empty bottle from the balcony table.

'Catacombs are fully booked,' she says. 'Turns out they weren't for hiding in. People went there for memorial meals, picnics with dead family and shit. Crazy right? You sure you're not hungry?'

For a moment, Meinir is seized by another urge to push her mother over the balcony. Taking the plastic cup, she remembers her friend Katy's explanation for the phenomenon. 'It's because we want to fly,' she'd said. 'It's that same childhood urge.'

'I suppose I could eat something,' says Meinir.

Elena rests a hand on Meinir's wrist, and although Meinir squirms at her mother's touch, she lets the weight of her mother's hand sink into the layers of her skin, until she can once again feel the steel of her bones, the flickering of her muscles, the throb and tingle of her spring-loaded hair.

Afterwards, grabbing her phone from the bedside table, she messages Dog.

best if i dont c u anymore

LiFE iS NOT A BUNCH OF FUCKiNG ROSES

The robin is the first dead thing Ellen has ever seen. One minute it's perched on one of the ash tree's upturned shoots, singing at full throttle; the next minute she's shot it through the chest.

'Gotcha!' screams Madison at Ellen's side. 'Noisy cunt.'

The robin has landed on the ground beside the footpath, a few inches from a freshly dug grave plot behind the girls. Ellen can't understand how it could have flown so far from the ash tree with its heart and belly blown into a thousand bloody pieces.

'Is it dead?' she asks Madison, her voice quivering. 'Did I kill it?'

Ellen hadn't meant to kill the robin. Madison made her do it, forcing the air pistol into her hand. Ellen throws up a splodge of watery orange sick that looks like bird shit as Madison kicks the bird into the grave plot.

'Life's not a bunch of fucking roses, Ellen.'

Their paths had crossed an hour earlier by accident. Ellen was taking a short cut through the old part of the cemetery on her way home from an errand to Londis, when Madison suddenly emerged from behind the electricity junction box near the cemetery exit.

'Oy, Ellen,' she'd yelled, jabbing a brown gnarly stick in Ellen's direction. 'You blankin' me again or what?'

Madison, who was a second cousin once removed on Ellen's father's side, lived in a row of council houses that lined the cemetery's northern perimeter. Like most of the kids on Elan Avenue, Madison rarely visited the old part of the cemetery that flanked Ellen's cul-de-sac. Instead, she and her band of hard-eyed friends, with their pale luminous skin, slug eyebrows, and dazzling hoop earrings, hung out by the battered wooden shelter near the north gate that looked to Ellen liked a burnt-out gazebo. Ellen hadn't seen Madison for over a year, which was strange considering they used to play together daily as kids.

'Didn't see you,' said Ellen. 'Sorry.'

'Yeah right,' said Madison.

Madison had shimmied up the waist-high railings that surrounded the junction box, arcing her leg over the top, still holding on to the stick. She was wearing a faded denim micro-skirt and grubby red and blue sliders, and as she swung her second leg over the railing, Ellen caught a flash of crimson gusset.

'Bet you poshos ain't never seen a gun before, ave ya?' said Madison.

Ellen soon realised that the stick was actually an air gun.

Madison shoved the gun into her mouth and mimed giving it a blow job, making pinched eerie sex noises as she sucked on the gun's squat brown barrel. A fake eyelash peeled away from her eyelid like rheum. Meanwhile, the vanilla ice cream tub from Londis was digging into Ellen's calf in a strange and removed way, as if her leg was not attached to her body, and she wondered whether Madison was about to blow her own head off. In English class, they'd read about The Wood of Suicides that existed in hell.

'Is it real?' Ellen said, trying to sound casual. 'The gun?'

'It's ex-police. Glock 17 air pistol. Uncle Eddie bought it in The Wilkie. You lot know jack shit.'

Uncle Eddie, Madison's stepfather, worked as a groundsman in the cemetery. Ellen's mother said he was always up to 'no good'. Madison wiped the gun on her sleeve; a gleaming trail of saliva seeped into her North Face down jacket.

'I've got to go. I need to be home by six,' said Ellen. 'I've got lifeguarding.'

Ellen was training to be a lifeguard at the municipal swimming pool. Tonight, they were completing their Gold Stage first aid training using a pool Rescue Dummy that weighed thirty kilos and was meant to mimic an unconscious body floating in water.

Madison shook her head from side to side.

'Lifeguarding,' said Madison. 'Fucking joke. If you know what's good for you, you'll come with me.'

After they'd made contact at the junction box, Ellen had followed Madison around the old part of the cemetery past the warden's lodge with the six-foot wall and through a tunnel of cypress trees lined on either side with ancient statues. Madison dragged the gun along the tree trunks as she walked, like a boy clanging a stick against school railings. Ellen's anxiety was at an all-time high. Where were they going? What was the gun for? But even as she imagined herself being gunned down by Madison in the tree tunnel and then splayed across one of the cemetery's huge tabletop tombstones, she nevertheless felt safer in the old part of the cemetery than in the newer part, where it seemed Madison was now taking her. To Ellen, the new part of the cemetery was a different country with different rules; there were no trees or fancy statues where you could hide.

'Eddie probably fucks this one in the ass,' said Madison, stopping abruptly. 'Looks young enough.'

At the end of the cypress tree tunnel was a life-sized weeping angel bent over a crumbling old ledger stone, her head tucked into the crook of her arm. A dark slice of face was just about visible through the crook of the angel's arm, revealing a pockmarked stone cheek and parted, lichen-stained lips.

'They played a porno vid in a funeral last week,' said Madison. 'It was in The Post. Bluetooth connected to someone's phone by mistake.'

'What do you mean?'

'Duh. Someone was watching porn on their phone, shit for brains,' said Madison. 'Cemetery's bluetooth picked up the signal. So, instead of getting a cheesy montage of memories and Celine Dion wailing like a fucking bitch, family got an eyeful of kiddie porn.'

Madison poked the airgun through the folds of the angel's gown into her ass crack, holding it like a cock, thrusting and moaning all the while.

'God,' said Ellen. 'That's so messed up.'

A house alarm sounded from somewhere up ahead, filtering down through the leaves of trees, interrupting Madison's performance for a second. Ellen became aware of other noises. A dog yapping. A hearse backfiring. The lurch of her own blood.

'Isn't this the statue we put lippy on,' she'd said, changing the subject. 'Remember? The Chanel Rouge I stole from my mother's dressing table. We took selfies.'

Madison stopped butt-fucking the angel. A prolonged silence caused Ellen to wonder whether she'd said something wrong. The weeping angel was missing a left hand and a wingtip, the sight of which made Ellen suddenly thrust her hands into the pocket of her hoodie.

'Was that before you bailed on me?' asked Madison, grinning weirdly. 'Before you thought you were too good for me?

'It wasn't like that,' said Ellen.

When Madison was ten, her gran Rosalie, who kept house for Dave the cemetery warden, stole power tools and a dog cage from the lodge's storage unit and then advertised them for sale on a local Gumtree site. When Ellen's parents found out about the theft, she was forbidden from playing with Madison.

'Whatever,' said Madison. 'Like I give a shit.'

By now they'd emerged from the tunnel into the new part of the cemetery. Everything was as Ellen had expected. A wide gravelled footpath with the feel of a dried-out riverbed led directly to the cemetery's north gate. Small stubby gravestones emerged from the grass here and there, like the exposed stumps of a once-submerged forest. The whole area was overlooked on one side by the houses on Elan Avenue and on the other by the crem and the steel works. Ellen felt as exposed as if she was naked.

'I want to teach you a life lesson,' said Madison. 'I want you to shoot something.'

At first, Ellen had tried to resist. But Madison had the same expression on her face as she'd had all those years ago when she'd told Ellen about the plague of cockroaches living under her gran's tiny bed in the lodge, as if she'd been let down by life in some horrible, irreversible way. The expression had since fermented into rage.

'I'm really sorry about everything Maddy,' said Ellen. 'It was my mother. She stopped me playing with you. She thought you were a—'

'Nah, you're just a coward,' interrupted Madison. 'And if you don't want everyone knowing what a chickenshit you are, you'll do what I say.'

Ellen's new Nike trainers sank into the footpath as she trudged after Madison towards the top gate. The gravel made a sickening bone-crunching noise underfoot. They passed the crem on their left, and then a couple of green metal sheds that had no obvious purpose, and Ellen thought she saw Madison's Uncle Eddie standing idly in what looked like a trench, looking intently in their direction. Although she could only see the top half of his body, the tapering shape of his head was familiar.

'He's always there, with his beady little peepers,' said Madison. 'Smug little asshole.'

Ellen didn't know who Madison was talking about. Uncle Eddie? But then she saw it: a robin. Perched on the cemetery's perimeter railing in front of the battered wooden bus shelter ahead. Madison raised the airgun to her right shoulder and pretended to fire at the robin. The robin disappeared into the uppermost branches of the only tree in this part of the cemetery: a forty-foot ash, the only surviving tree from an outbreak of ash dieback. Ellen remembered her father saying that the tree had been there for three hundred years, maybe longer.

'Uncle Eddie feeds it every day. Thinks it's his fucking mate. I want you to shoot its head off.'

As if on cue, the robin began to sing. A crazy, frightened roll of defiant warbling, chest puffed out like a fighter, wind blustering his orange feathers to reveal a dark circle of down.

'I don't know how to,' Ellen said. 'I don't want to.'

'Nobody cares what any of us fucking want.' said Madison. 'Toughen the fuck up.'

Pivoting around to face Ellen, Madison stabbed the butt of the air gun into her cousin's stomach, twisting it up into her kidneys.

The robin made a phut phut kind of sound.

'Aim for the bird with the sights,' she said, handing Ellen the gun. 'Bring the gun up so the notch is level with the top of the post, then fire.'

The dense composite silence that consumes the air after Ellen has fired the gun is like nothing she has experienced before, as if somebody has piled silence upon silence upon silence. Already, she knows that everything will be different from now on; this white noise will be with her forever; she'll have to learn to live with it in the same way somebody else might live with tinnitus.

Madison is meanwhile ranting on about Uncle Eddie, who has since disappeared from the trench where he was standing.

'Pigs nabbed everyone's phone for the investigation after the porno screening. Eddie blames the Bluetooth system, says it's a joke, council spunking hard-earned taxpayer's money on dead people.'

They arrive back at the weeping angel statue that Madison butt-fucked with the gun. Madison throws the airgun at Ellen.

You carry it now,' she says. 'It's killing me.'

The dead robin is assuming mass in Ellen's mind, adding visuals to the spongy white noise. Ellen wants to ask Madison what she was doing skulking around by the electricity junction box earlier. Why did she make her kill the robin? But something about the way Madison has by now positioned herself on the ledger stone, the way she's lying there, prostrate, with her hair hanging in separated dirty blond strands over the side of the stone like the weeping angel's hair, reminds Ellen of something from way back. Once, she and Madison had stayed in the cemetery until closing time, lying top-to-toe on a chest tomb, as though they were on a little kids' sleepover. It was Madison's tenth birthday, a few months before Rosalie stole the power tools and the dog cage, and Ellen's parents had allowed her to stay out until dusk. Madison said that she missed her real dad, who'd fallen forty foot through a factory roof whilst fitting scaffolding six months earlier. Ellen shared out the red velvet Disney cupcakes her mum had made, and Madison said that it would be cool if everybody else in the world fell asleep for a year, except for them, like in the Sleeping Beauty story.

Ellen caught the airgun and said nothing.

'They'll probably find it on his moby though, the kiddie porn,' says Madison, getting up from the stone. 'Whenever my mum's out of the house he puts porn on in the living room, not kiddie porn or anything, just regular hardcore, fake snuff shit. Last week he asked me to watch it with him, fucking creeper.'

Ellen doesn't know what to say.

'I'm sorry,' she says, lamely.

Ellen hands the gun back to Madison at the junction box by the old cemetery gate, where she now sees that somebody has spray-painted a row of spouting cocks and the words NO GOD in bright neon lettering. Ellen's arm is so numb right now after pulling the trigger on the robin that she doubts she'll be able to tow the sinking Rescue Dummy to safety later on.

'Christ. We used to play hide and seek behind this stupid box,' says Madison, sliding the gun into her pocket. 'I come here to smoke weed with Jamal.'

'Oh, right,' says Ellen.

'Oh, right?' says Madison.

'Just wondered why you were here is all.'

'Get over yourself. Please. I wasn't here cos of you bro, if that's what you're thinking. Though I won't lie, when I saw your smug daddy's little girl face coming down the path, skipping like we were in fucking Oz, I totally wanted to wipe the smile off, no offence.'

Madison laughs dryly and lights a fag. From where she's standing, Ellen can see the blue gable end of their house, and a builder on an extendable ladder reattaching a fascia board that had flown off the side in Storm Malcolm. She no longer belongs here with Madison, of course: they were no longer friends or even family. Madison was a total psycho. And yet Ellen knows that her parents were also partly to blame. In banishing Madison from their daughter's life all those years ago, they had acted unjustly and unkindly. But it was fear of, course. It was always fear, and fear was as understandable as love.

'Anyway, enjoy lifeguarding or piano or whatever else posho bollocks you get up to,' says Madison. 'Oh, and try not to drown yourself yeah, it was only a fucking robin.'

'Why did you make me kill it?' Ellen asks, finally.

'Grow up,' says Madison. 'You killed it yourself.'

mETASTASiSEd

Clive is kneeling in front of the aquarium's isolation tank, adjusting the settings on the filter, when his sister-in-law returns to the conservatory.

'Andrew won't fuck me,' she says. 'Because of the cancer.'

Rhiannon's words bounce between the neurons in Clive's brain like balls in a pinball machine, refusing to remain still. By the time they settle into sentences, Rhiannon is sitting on the wicker sofa by the yucca, having helped herself to a bottled lager from the fridge. Not for the first time, Clive observes the androgynous lines of her body, which make her seem younger than her forty-five years, the airy quality of her strawberry-blond hair.

'I'm sorry,' he says, afraid to look now.

'I want to feel alive again,' she says. 'Maybe you can help?'

Clive releases an inchoate 'oh'. A sudden erection tents out the fabric of his utility trousers. His last erection was over a year ago, when he ventured into town to bulk-buy vitamins from a health store. In the window of a nearby shop, a naked mannequin with tuberous swellings for genitalia filled him with such strange sensations, such powerful currents of longing, he was forced to hide his ensuing boner behind a carrier bag.

Rhiannon rises from the sofa and saunters towards him. She halts mere inches away, places a finger on his mouth, and gently presses it into the ridge above his lip.

'Shh,' she says, stroking the arc of his cock. 'It'll be ok.'

She'd first come to him a month and a half earlier, suddenly appearing in his garden like a ghost, a carrier bag of strange dark shapes swinging from her wrist. Clive was too busy jet washing the conservatory to notice her approach.

'Brought you some stones for your fish tank,' she said. 'Heard you keep fish.'

He'd jumped back in shock at her voice, dropping the jet washer's trigger gun. Pellets of freezing water flayed his shins.

'You ok?' she said. 'Sorry. Anyway. I was on a bike ride. They were piled up on the verge of a grave. I thought it was a waste, so—'

He hadn't seen Rhiannon or his brother in years, even though they lived less than a mile away, so the obvious thing would have been to enquire about their wellbeing, say something casual like, 'long time no see,' but he couldn't get the words out.

'It's nothing,' he replied, floundering as he accepted the carrier bag. 'We'll have to wash off the parasites. I'll get a bucket.'

When he returned from the outhouse with the bucket, Rhiannon was waiting for him by the sink in the kitchen. Clive continued to act as if there was nothing unusual about the way she'd re-appeared after all this time, with unsolicited gravel for his tank; having levered herself over the gate to gain entry. He remembered the day in the car park, twenty years earlier, when she'd also approached him out of the blue. But no, it didn't bear thinking about.

'Hope you left some on the grave,' he said, as she helped him wash the stones in the bucket. 'Poor dead guy'll freeze his nuts off.'

He spoke out of turn when he was nervous.

'Tits,' she said, emphatically. 'Freeze her tits off.'

Their skin touched under the water in the bucket. A crop of small, hard goosebumps sprung into life on her hairy, tanned forearm.

'It was a woman's grave.'

It wasn't until her second visit to the conservatory that she told him about the cancer.

Clive was attending to a sliver of soft rot on the door sill, replacing it with fresh wood, when he spotted her peeking around the perimeter wall, wrapped in a belted coat with a red velvet fringe. Although the coat concealed her body, he could see that she was thicker around the waist. With a sickening feeling, he wondered if she was pregnant.

'I was passing by again,' she said. 'Do the fish like their stones?'

'Better ask the little bastards,' he laughed nervously.

He made her a cup of tea, scalding his hand in the steam.

'I love the one with the wonky stripe,' he heard her yell.

It was Clive's friend Steff who suggested he buy an aquarium, claiming it helped reduce blood pressure. Clive's blood pressure was a solid 140 over 90, making him pre-hypertensive, but the medical benefits appealed to him less than the challenge itself. 'There's a million and one things to learn,' Steff had said. 'The chemistry of the water, day and night cycles, biological balance.' Over the summer, Clive had upgraded to a twenty-one-gallon aquarium, adding eight neon tetras, five guppies, and three zebra danios. He was still researching the benefits of a bettafish.

When he returned to the conservatory with tea, Rhiannon was scrooched down behind the aquarium, her face distorted by the ten-millimetre-thick glass.

'The kink in the stripe means she's a girl,' he said. 'Watch.'

Using the gizmo that worked the conservatory blinds, Clive drew the blinds half-way down with a showy flourish he instantly regretted. In the new dark of the conservatory, the tetra stripes glowed vividly in the tank: red and blue and back to red. Afterwards, she emerged from behind the tank and stood beside him, closer than ever, unruly threads of hair springing out and brushing against his unshaven cheek.

'I've got cancer, Clive,' she said, suddenly turning to him. 'Ovarian.'

Clive didn't know whether to open or completely close the blinds. When he scanned the gizmo for inspiration, he found his brain had lost the capacity to decipher the buttons and symbols. Throwing the gizmo to the other side of the conservatory, the blinds suddenly shot up with a tearing sound.

'No. No. What the fuck are you talking about?'

'It's Stage 4,' she said.

The impact of the flung gizmo had cracked the conservatory window. Following the fresh fissure with his eye, Clive imagined tracing his fingers across the contours of Rhiannon's abdomen. It was grotesque, he knew, depraved even, but the truth was that a small part of him was relieved that it was a tumour and not a pregnancy. (It made him angry to think of his brother spewing hot thick fluid into her body.)

'It metastasized. From my breasts,' she said.

Now, less than a fortnight after he'd first learned of her diagnosis, five weeks after she'd given him the gravel, he follows her up the stairs to his bedroom. From behind she looks totally normal: the fringe of her cardigan swinging playfully.

'Last room at the end of the hall,' he says.

'I love that I still turn you on, after all these years,' she says, turning to him. 'Andrew sleeps in the guest room. He says it's because he snores, because he doesn't want to keep me awake. The truth is he can't bear my body.'

Terrified of letting her down, Clive checks his cock for signs of waning, wondering whether he should have taken the Viagra he'd ordered online.

'Can't believe *you* still fancy me,' he says.

But after they blissfully orgasm, she turns away from him towards the bedroom window, and Clive worries that the intervention hasn't worked. And yet her voice is bright and cheerful.

'That was *the* best sex,' she says, throwing off the duvet. 'But I've got to go now, Clive. Thanks.'

'Stay,' he says, elated. 'What's the rush?'

'I have an appointment. At the doctor.'

Clive watches her screw the stem of a silver hoop through her earlobe. When she reaches for her underwear, his eyes travel to the angel wings tattoo which has replaced her breasts. She hadn't mentioned the mastectomy beforehand, and so naturally, it had been a shock to him. But not in the way he might have imagined.

'So, I take it you like the tattoo then?' she says.

'It's fantastic,' he says.

During their lovemaking, Clive had been so mesmerized by the magnificent detail of the tattoo; the meticulous rendering of the underside of each wing; feathers shaded in the deepest black he'd ever seen; any anxieties about his performance had soon faded. But it was more than that too. Each wing seemed to beat before his eyes. And although Clive knew he was looking at a tattoo, it was as if he was in the company of something—or someone—special, as if he was witnessing a transformation: as though Rhiannon was an angel, or god.

'So, shouldn't we tell Andrew?' he says, rising from the bed. 'About us, I mean.'

Rhiannon eases her legs into her jeans.

'I'm dying, Clive. Remember? Why cause problems?'

Clive's older brother Andrew worked as an auditor for an accounting firm. On the rare occasions they saw each other, at a family event, a wedding maybe, the tension between them baffled Clive. And yet his suggestion that they tell Andrew about the affair wasn't motivated by animosity, or rivalry, but by a sense of duty towards Rhiannon: a belief that the relationship could be redemptive for both of them.

'But you're alive now. You're more alive than me.'

'It's not enough Clive,' she says. 'It's too late.'

Seized by panic and regret, Clive can only watch impotently from his side of the bed as she coils a long rainbow scarf around her throat, as she teases out a length of trapped hair.

'I need to ask you something,' he says. 'It's important.'

'Yes?' she says.

Suddenly afraid of her response, he turns his head towards the window.

'That time we were in the car. Twenty years ago. Did it mean anything to you?'

Clive remembered the exchange between them not only as an event from the past, but as something that was still playing out, something that hadn't yet been resolved, something he could change, if he only knew how. It had happened in the car park outside *The Captain's Wife*, where they'd attended a family dinner to celebrate his father's sixtieth. Clive had returned to his car, the beat-up Renault with the brown leather seats, to retrieve his phone, when he saw Rhiannon walking towards him across the car park. She slid into the passenger seat and kissed him. He was so startled by her actions, so overcome by an exhilarating kinetic energy that he immediately proposed they drive away together.

'I'm married, Clive,' she'd said. 'I'm sorry. I shouldn't have.'

He could still taste her lips to this day. The strangest, most enchanting kiss. Strange because she'd kept her eyes open throughout: as if she couldn't bear to miss a single second of his reaction. Enchanting because she tasted like the windfall apples from his gran's garden in Tycoch. As she'd fumbled with the door handle of the Renault, Clive noticed how close he'd parked to the sea wall; how, if a tsunami hit, they'd be instantly annihilated.

'Yes of course it meant something, but, well—' she says, faltering now, wrapping herself in her cardigan. 'It was a long time ago, Clive.'

'It's been twenty years, there hasn't been anyone else like you,' he says, surprising himself with his assertiveness, his directness.

'Why do you think you never found anybody?'

He shrugs, wishing he knew the answer. Over the years, there were women whose company Clive had enjoyed, but none sustained his interest.

'With Donna, I could barely get an erection.'

Following Rhiannon out to the landing, Clive still couldn't understand what she saw in him, when, by any conventional measure, his brother was far more successful, far better-looking, confident. Was it simply that his desire for her provided her with the validation she so desperately needed, offering proof that she was still a woman, still relevant, still alive?

'I want to see you again,' he says, as they reach the conservatory.

'It doesn't make any sense,' she says.

She leans in slowly, as if to kiss him goodbye, before suddenly withdrawing. When she reaches the gate, silently mouthing the word 'thanks', the fact that she knows the code for the padlock is too much for him to bear. He is about to give chase, beg her to stay and explain, when she disappears behind the gate.

At the funeral, six weeks later, he remains as confused as ever. The casket stays in place at the end of the service, instead of being lowered, and the crematorium curtains remain open, details that only increases his disorientation, his sense that there is something unfinished about their relationship.

Afterwards, he waits on the kerb of a stranger's gravestone until everyone else has departed, until a column of coral-tinted smoke rises from the smokestack. Knowing the smoke and ash is—was—Rhiannon, Clive springs into motion. He needs to see and touch and taste what is left of her. But by the time he reaches the crematorium, the smoke is so swiftly dispersing that he feels nothing but a rankling dissatisfaction when he inhales it into his lungs.

A man hurries across his path, jangling keys.

'We shut at six, mate,' he yells.

After the funeral Clive volunteers for overtime at the warehouse to keep busy. When his line manager yells at him to 'condense' the end-of-line stock to create space for new products, Clive can't help but think about Rhiannon's cremated body condensed forever into a jar, all the while fantasising about strangling his manager to death.

Meanwhile, at home, maintenance issues mount up. The polycarbonate roof windows of the conservatory have started to warp; the crack in the window has widened its vitreous web. Clive notices other things too. Plaster fraying around exposed pipes in the utility room; a sour smell maturing in the shower strainer. One day, whilst reattaching damp wallpaper to the alcove in his bedroom, he notices a set of keys on the floor by his bed. A green tassel key ring. Rhiannon's keys. Climbing down the ladder to investigate, his feet plunge into the carpet and sink further and further, as if a gaping sinkhole has given way.

His only respite is the fish tank, which instantly calms him. On a whim he upgrades to a vast cube aquarium and purchases a translucent Golden Mystery Snail to clear algae. But within a day of setting the whole thing up, the snail has already scaled the aquarium walls seeking escape, triggering in Clive an overpowering desolate feeling he cannot escape. He falls asleep on the sofa, unable to face the stairs.

When he wakes, something has changed. At first it feels as though there's been a change in atmospheric pressure; his chest feels oddly weighted down. It takes him a little while longer to realise that the change is, however, acoustic. The aquarium's new filter box is producing a bizarre, intermittent rattling noise, a wet crackling he would normally associate with laboured breathing. The snail is more than halfway up the glass wall, his grey foot like an eye, whilst the rest of the water is as empty and motionless as those freezing depths of sea where nothing moves.

Assuming the fish have been drawn into the filter by an excessively strong current, Clive switches the power off and disassembles the tubes. He brings the intake tube up to his mouth. But instead of blowing to dislodge any blockage, he unwittingly sucks. In a fizzing cold heap, something dissolves on the back of his tongue, slipping down his oesophagus into darkness. The next few minutes are a blur. Fleeing the conservatory, he spits the paste into a shrub by the driveway, where he watches numbly as it slides off a leaf, but even after he's rinsed his mouth out in the kitchen, and reintroduced the fish trapped in the filter back into the aquarium, the taste is still there, on the edge of his senses, taking shape. He counts the fish again, and then again. The tetra with the kink is no longer there.

An hour later he arrives at Rhiannon's house, with her keys stuffed into his dressing gown. With the tetra gone, the tetra she loved, it's as if some final living link to her has been severed, a link he must somehow restore. Instead of providing Clive with the closure he thought he so needed, the loss of the tetra has simply compounded his need to connect with Rhiannon one more time.

At first, he wants only to imagine the life he and Rhiannon might have had together (if only he had been man enough, bullish enough). He doesn't plan to venture further than the stone steps at the end of the driveway. But with no car outside, and no one at home, he feels compelled to explore.

Climbing over the side gate at the top of the steps, he peers through the first ground floor window into a sleek lounge with minimal décor, a modern modular sofa, illuminated twigs beside a fake, chimney-less stove. The sight is so disconcerting, so unlike how he imagined Rhiannon might furnish her house, it's as if he's misunderstood something vast and fundamental. Moving to the next window he triggers a motion sensor and quickly retreats.

But then, as he's turning to leave, he notices a building at the bottom of the garden. Fingering the keys in his pocket, one key is larger than the rest, a single tooth on the shaft, Clive suddenly remembers Rhiannon talking about a garage she was planning to turn into a studio as soon as she quit her job in the probation service. The building was most definitely a garage. Wading through knee-length grass towards a door hidden behind rampant ivy, he slips the key into the lock.

Slowly, almost theatrically, the lights flicker on one by one, illuminating different zones in the garage. Closest to Clive is a supermarket trolley stuffed with various accessories: the rainbow scarf he recognises, a battered panama hat. Behind that, suspended from loops of climbing rope, hang countless colourful dresses. Clive wonders if, somewhere amongst her belongings, is the explanation of why she'd come to him. But as he searches for clues, a way back into her life, his actions dislodge a sheet of paper from a pile of paperbacks: a sign written in his brother's straight-up-and-down hand.

All Items 50p o.n.o.

Andrew was selling her stuff. Disposing of her.

Sinking to the floor, the strength in his legs depleted, Clive knows he must save Rhiannon all over again. But how? Perhaps he could offer to buy all her stuff. Confront Andrew. As he examines the zones once again, clueless as to how to proceed, his attention is drawn to an object at the back.

At first glance it looks like a vase. Not an ordinary vase like the ones on the trestle table behind the dresses, but a special vase: a vase with a purpose he has yet to decipher.

He steps a little closer to the object, into a draught circulating the garage's roller shutter doors. The vase has an almost human quality, which reminds him of those naked, forlorn-looking tailors dummies. Kneeling to take a look, Clive tightens the sash of his dressing gown sash against the draught whipping up.

The vase is not a vase but an urn.

When he returns to his conservatory at around midnight, with Rhiannon's urn in a bright shopper purloined at the last minute from the back of the garage, the fish seem particularly active, pulsing through the water with impatient zeal, as if the thrill of being released from their temporary filter prison has given them a new lease of life. Switching off the floor lamp so that the fish are able to sleep, Clive gently unscrews the urn's lid. Inside, he expects to see a fine grey substance, like soot, but the cremains are pale and creamy, with an almost radioactive lime-green tinge.

When he was in his twenties, Clive smoked a lot of weed. After crushing the cannabis, the bottom of the grinder would always contain a strange sticky substance, a glimmering resin called kief.

Rhiannon's cremains look like kief.

It doesn't take Clive long to find a dealer. Within the hour, he has picked up an eighth from his old school friend Micky who still lives above the 'Something's Fishy' chip shop on the estate, and brought it back to the conservatory, where, with a sweet-scary feeling rising in his abdomen, he rolls his roach and prepares his Rizla.

Smoking Rhiannon won't save her, of course, he knows that much, neither will it unlock any of her secrets, but after the visceral shock of the garage sale, Clive feels a sudden need to liberate her from the bland, stultifying confinement of the urn. And if they connect in the process, all the better.

Initially his plan is to roll a normal joint: two pinches of weed, a scattering of cremains. But in the context of the fantastical, cone-shaped spliffs from his youth, the small, unrolled joint on the coffee table seems pitiful, hopeless, demeaning. Sprinkling two much larger pinches of weed on to the Rizla now, more at one end than the other to create a cone, Clive blankets the concoction in Rhiannon's soft cremains, as if he's sprinkling it with hundreds and thousands, cake toppers. Finally, he lifts the paper, pinches it together, and starts rolling.

The first few puffs are disorienting. Clive watches his rangy legs arc towards him in peculiar segments, like spiders' legs, as if he's seeing himself from inside the aquarium; his big hands, cartoonish and frightening, flapping around the flaccid joint. Why in the actual fuck was he sucking up dead people? Was it any wonder he didn't have a girlfriend or wife? But those were the voices of his detractors. His brother. His asshole line manager. Donna.

Inhaling deeper, and deeper still, it occurs to him that nobody has ever been this intimate with Rhiannon. Nobody has felt her entirety between their fingertips. Nobody has been so close and personal to the extraordinary phosphates and salts that were once her bones. As the epiphany breaks free of his mind and flows through his blood, Clive swallows swirling Technicolor visions of spiralling smoke, which intricately reform in his lungs as tendrils of Rhiannon's beautiful hair, as delicate feathers that flourish into mighty angel wings, as if he's bringing her back to life.

Drawing the last of her cremains into his mouth, Clive holds his breath a little longer. Rhiannon's velvety smoke body curls up post-coitally on his tongue. She rubs her spreading smoky ass against his palate. She reaches way back into the cavern of his throat. She licks his gums, caresses every part of the inside of his cheeks, sucks his teeth, filling his whole head with a taste even more tantalising than the brief, stolen kiss in the Renault. As he breathes out the last of her into the air, returning her to the palliative morning light filtering through the blinds, the fish in the aquarium burrow out of their sandy sleep holes and, one by one, teeter slowly into life.

BACKSLIDERS

The trainee apostle takes Laura to his trailer at the back of the caravan site.

'It's super important we pray with people once they're saved, Laura,' he says.

He leads Laura up the steps of his trailer to a cramped decking area, where a huge model of a T-Rex made of rusting scrap metal, draped in fairy lights and a Hawaiian boa, towers over a plastic chair and small table.

'I'll make us a Thank You Jesus smoothie before we start. Holy Spirit raises your core temperature.'

Laura, who used to think that being saved meant being yanked out of a towering inferno by a ripped firefighter or being dragged out of the water by a lifeguard, can't be sure that she's been saved, even though she still has a new shivery feeling in her belly from the service in the Fellowship. All the same, she likes the idea of being singled out for something special.

'You got anything else, Nathan?' she says. 'Gran lets me have Lambrini on Fridays.'

Nathan opts for a long look that passes through Laura's body like radiation.

'The soul needs more than alcohol, Laura.'

Guiding her into a kitchenette overlooking the cockle beds, Nathan pours a carton of sweetened almond milk into a blender, adding bananas and a powder that looks like Agent Orange. Arranged on a rack above the draining board are sachets of hemp powder, matcha powder, spirulina.

'God's work is thirsty work, Laura. Did you hear the parable about the woman in the well?

A solar-powered angel toy with a rubbed-out mouth makes a buzzing noise on the worktop, bobbing its head around like a psych patient.

'Sounds like a horror flick,' says Laura. 'You know, like The Woman in Black or Girl On A Train. It's always a …'

The trainee apostle hits the on switch on the blender, cutting off Laura mid-speech. The buzz of the angel toy gives way to the dental-drill shriek of the blender.

'She was a whore,' says Nathan. 'When Jesus went up to her, she was by herself, drawing water out of a well. She was so shocked to be approached by a man, a total no-no in those days, she told Jesus to go fuck himself.'

Prickles form on Laura's neck as Nathan speaks. Were trainee apostles allowed to swear or to say whore? She thinks of the whores working the alley behind gran's flat. Laura always wondered what it would be like to be one of them. Anonymous but at the same time desired. There but not there. Nathan hands her the smoothie in a cloudy pint glass.

'Do you know what Jesus said to her?' he says.

Laura shakes her head as she drinks.

'If you knew who I was, lady, you'd be the one asking me for a drink.'

Laura follows Nathan down a narrow corridor towards the back of the trailer.

'The blackout curtain in the master bedroom is super good for praying. Satan uses daylight to distract.'

The corridor is way longer than Laura would have expected, with closed doors on either side and a stink of fish raining down from a bulb. Laura's smartphone goes off in her jeans pocket.

'Through here,' says Nathan. 'And put your phone off.'

The door to Nathan's bedroom is a thick, rust brown curtain with flowers. The only light in the room comes from a dolphin-shaped night light clamped to a single futon base, which projects a pale, watery rainbow on the wallpaper. A poster of a unicorn leaping over a deep ravine is sellotaped to the wall opposite the futon.

'Love the rainbow light,' says Laura. 'My mate Jared bought the same one in Pride.'

'Gay pride conflicts with God's view of sexuality, Laura. For a male to lie with a male is an abomination.'

'Jared's a really good bloke though. He used to live in a refugee camp in Turkey. Came here with his brother Falak two years ago. He fixed my gran's gate.'

'What can Fellowship have in common with darkness Laura?' he says, looking at her through the slits of his eyes, waiting for an answer.

Laura shrugs and sits down on the futon, wondering where to rest her glass. The smoothie is the same colour as piss turns when you've left it for too long in the bowl.

'You remind me of her,' says Nathan, suddenly. 'The woman in the well. You have a thirsty soul. You crave things.'

Laura isn't sure whether being compared to the woman in a Bible story is a complement. She can smell Nathan's aftershave more clearly now, not only because of the proximity of their bodies in the small airless room, but because his sweat makes the high notes stand out. When she'd first met Nathan a few hours earlier, at the Fellowship on Charnelwood Road, he was sat on a low wall outside the front door, in a bridal dress, veil, and long train. A sandwich board that read 'You Can't Get from A Man or Woman What You Can Only Get from God' hung around his neck. Laura wondered whether he was trans or non-binary. There was a trans in school who scared the living shit out of her. But then again, he also looked like one of those people they locked in stocks in medieval times, the bridal train curled around his feet like a chain. No sooner had Laura started feeling sorry for him than the 'g' and 'd' consonants in the word God assumed weight and mass in her mind. She noticed he was handsome, with blond hair clipped into a burr cut like velvet.

'You're the type who could backslide quite easily, Laura,' he says now.

Taking the glass form her, and resting it on the floor next to a bass guitar in the corner of the room, he leans over her body to reach for the dolphin light, fumbling for the off switch on the cord.

'We've got no time to waste.'

When the room is dark, apart from a seam of daylight seeping in under the door curtain, Nathan paces the bedroom like a big cat in a zoo enclosure. Punches the wall. Then, as if he's suddenly hot, he takes his hoodie off, throws it on to a fake prickly pear cactus in the other corner. It takes Laura a moment to register that underneath the hoodie he is naked.

'Take your blouse off too,' he says. 'Clothes are an obstacle to achieving full spiritual connection.'

Laura isn't wearing a blouse. She is wearing a cropped T-shirt on loan to her from her older sister, Kim, who moved out of their gran's flat six months ago to move in with her boyfriend, Tyler. The T-shirt has a picture of an evil clown from an old timey horror film and smells of Kim's knock-off 'Daisy' perfume. Laura doesn't want to wash the T-shirt in case the scent of her sister disappears.

'Skin to skin praying will allow God's divine healing energy to flow freely,' says Nathan. 'There's no time to waste. The enemy could already have infiltrated.'

Laura pictures a scrap metal T-Rex version of Satan coming up the steps of the trailer, a flashing snake around his rusty neck. She imagines the no-face wind-up angel toy from the kitchenette flying down the corridor like a cockroach. Sensing her hesitation, Nathan kicks the cactus pot.

'I'm starting to wonder why you even came to the fellowship, Laura? I took you for someone more mature. Braver. But ...'

The smell of aftershave has metabolised into something more like a taste than a smell. Medicinal. It collects in Laura's throat like powder. The truth was that Laura didn't know exactly why she'd gone to the Fellowship, except that it was something different to do with her time. When the flyer had come through the door of gran's flat, a week earlier, 'Who Else Knows How Lonely and Scared You Are?' emblazoned across the cover, the words spoke to her. Also, she liked the artwork. But Nathan was right. She hadn't gone to the Fellowship for exclusively spiritual reasons, whatever spiritual meant.

'Sorry,' she says.

She takes off her top as requested, relieved that the room is so dark. The roll of whiter-than-white fat around her waist makes her look like a glow worm. Last week, a boy in Year 10 had called her a fupa, which was short for Fat Upper Pussy Area. She hates, too, her sticky-out belly button, the crater of scarred tissue on her upper arm from the BCG, her lumpy arms in general. For a minute, she worries that the angle of her body, the rhythm of her breathing, will alert Nathan to the possibility that she might not actually be saved, whilst another part of her just wants to go home. Looking over, she notices Nathan has lowered his head. His head looks like Christ's head on the cross in the picture in gran's living room.

'Lord Jesus. Thank you Jesus. Thank you for saving Laura from the sin and lust and deceit in her heart. Make her as thirsty for your juicy word as the whore by the well. Shoot your loving mercy into the channels of her body Lord Jesus. Hallelujah.'

Closing her eyes, Laura focusses on Nathan's words. Was she as sinful as he claimed? The other night, after receiving the flyer about the Fellowship, Laura had had a random fantasy about the Angel Gabriel being sent by the Lord to impregnate her. She'd left her bedroom window open that night so that the angel could slide under the sash like the T2 in Terminator and turn into a real flesh and blood boy. In the same week, she'd given Jared's brother Falak a hand job in the alley.

When she opens her eyes, Nathan is sitting beside her on the futon, holding something in his hand. A rectangle of colourful fabric.

'Put this on,' he says. 'There's still too much light pollution.'

The rectangle of fabric is one of those bandanas Laura has seen surfer boys wearing on the beach. When Nathan ties it around her eyes to create a blindfold, the pressure of his hand takes her back to the service at the Fellowship, where he'd lain his hands on her in prayer.

She was sitting next to the heavily tattooed mother of a boy with Down's Syndrome at the time. Nathan was playing the guitar on a wooden dais at the front of the hall, leading the congregation in a song called 'You Gave Away Your Majesty', having by then swopped his bridal veil for a grey Adidas hoodie and combat trousers. Laura sang along with the lyrics, which were about God ridding people of their shame. The hall crackled like grass catching fire. Individuals made their way down the aisles, toppling from time to time, like toddlers trying out their new legs. The mother of the Down's Syndrome boy screamed 'Take Me Jesus, I Bloody Love You.' Laura must have been out of it for a while; she had a habit of falling into trances, especially when she was stressed. When she emerged from her trance, Nathan was kneeling to her side.

'We pray that you move inside our sister Laura tonight, Lord Jesus.'

It was something she'd seen Dynamo doing on TV, guessing people's names. Nathan brought her hand to his abdomen. A pulsing energy passed directly from his skin into hers, swarming through her like a flash flood, occupying every part of her. It was a bit like a scene in an old film she and Kim once watched, called Cocoon, where an alien fucks a human in a swimming pool, regenerating the human's life force. It wasn't fucking in a strictly human sense, but it was similar. The alien had an aura of light around their body, which was their life force made visible. When the light whooshed around through the human, they convulsed like they were having an orgasm.

'Adam and Eve were naked in the Garden of Eden,' says Nathan, tightening the bandana. 'There's no shame in it.'

Through the bandana, daylight is still visible under the door curtain. To the right of the curtain is the plastic cactus. Beside the cactus is a pair of trainers with massive lips, a box of Andrex tissues, an empty blue WKD bottle. Normal, reassuring everyday stuff. Outside the trailer, kids are kicking a ball about.

'Don't be scared,' says Nathan. 'It's God's will.'

Nathan kneels in front of her on the floor, resting each of his palms on her shoulders.

'Lord Jesus, may this sanctified flesh of mine be a conduit for your love. Lord Jesus. May the force of your righteous mercy flow like a river into Laura, not the measly dribble of love you sent her in the service Lord, no offence Lord, but a purifying mega-tsunami, purging her blood of Satan's load.'

Nathan groans like a woman in childbirth. The words lord and Jesus and hallelujah are lost in a gibberish of pulverized consonants.

You're hurting my shoulders actually Nathan,' says Laura, when Nathan presses into her shoulders too hard.

'God's force is working through me in tongues, Laura,' he says.

Looking back on the event, Laura can't remember precisely when Nathan brought up the subject of armpit sex. But around midway through the praying in tongues, he stops to tell her that God has one more instruction for them.

'It's only happened to me once before. This level of clarity in the messaging. God is working overtime to secure your future in his Kingdom, Laura. He loves you like a father. But his final revelation will only be revealed to me when I'm free of the distractions of flesh.'

Laura can't help thinking that if God's love is like a father's love, then this was a huge waste of time. The last time she and Kim saw their real father was at a meeting in a council office arranged for them by the social worker. Since then, he'd gone to live in Prestatyn.

'Actually. Maybe we could do it another time Nath,' she says.

A football smacks the window so hard the trailer lurches forwards like a boat. Nathan leaps up from the futon.

'Stay,' he says, when she tries to follow him out of the bedroom, having lifted the blindfold moments earlier. 'Your soul is still in grave mortal danger.'

Through the pane of thin glass that is the bedroom window, Laura sees him shouting at the group of twelve-year-olds kicking a ball in the car park. His back is turned to her, she can't see his face, but the expressions on the faces of the twelve-year-olds reminds Laura of the reaction shots you got in horror films, as if they've been spooked in some unimaginable way.

When he returns to the trailer, he is agitated. He duct tapes the curtains to the wall, and blocks the light from the hallway with a blanket. A series of raised stripes on his inner forearm that Laura hasn't noticed before gleam in the dark of the room.

'The inside of the body is a temple for the Holy Spirit. But the outside's OK' he says, randomly, without turning.

Laura doesn't know what he means.

'Outside the body. So, If I come in your armpit it's fine. It's not a sin.'

'Come?' she says.

He turns and stares straight into her.

'The Lord wants me to masturbate.'

Nathan kneels down and fiddles with his fly. The twelve raised stripes on his forearm remind Laura of the scars that Kim's friend Sugar has from cutting.

'My armpit is hairy as fuck though. Kim took the Veet. I could come next week instead? I'd prefer that. I could -'

'You took your blindfold off, Laura,' he interrupts, without looking up. 'You need to focus on praying not on looks. I can't do this without your help. It's a commandment from God.'

Laura slips the bandana back on.

'You're sitting way too high up,' he says.

He climbs on to the futon behind her, rests a palm on her shoulder to steady himself. She hears the rustling of trouser fabric, exasperated outbreaths. Wiry hairs from his chest touch her back.

'Open your arm a bit, for chrissakes' he says.

Afterwards, he takes her home in his camper van, which is airbrushed with depictions of the Milky Way and the moon, with added angels and impossible horses. The Moon has the face of an angel cherub like the face in the Teletubbies sun.

'Noah's brother Onan spilled his seed on the floor rather than impregnate his dead brother's wife. It was thoughtful. A mark of respect. The Bible doesn't forbid masturbation,' says Nathan, after a fairly long silence. 'In case you're wondering, Laura.'

They drive across the common land that separates the peninsula from the town, passing the tiny airport Laura has never seen planes landing in. When he'd moved into her armpit in the trailer, it was a strange silent affair, with hardly any movement on his part, just the sense of him burrowing into the recesses of her armpit, getting smaller not harder, and then ejaculating in a cold, small trickle on her back. She'd felt strangely removed from the situation, as if it was happening to somebody else, which was the opposite of how she'd felt in the church. Afterwards, when he was zipping up his fly, she checked the notifications on her phone. Kim had sent a scan picture of the baby she was expecting at Christmas. The baby looked a bit like an alien, but in a good way. The more Laura focused on the silvery white lines of real live bone in the scan image, arcing upwards along the baby's back around her skull, the more she felt as if nothing Nathan said or did really mattered.

'I wasn't thinking anything,' says Laura.

They turn off the common into the estate, passing the skinny woman who always pushed an empty supermarket trolley around the playground, and then, as they pass the Londis, Jared and Falak and their friends.

'Drop me off here,' she says, when they get to the bus stop at the corner of gran's street. 'I'll walk the rest of the way.'

Nathan pulls into the bus stop as requested.

'I'm sorry I couldn't save you,' he says, parking up. 'I tried. The Lord tried.'

'You said I was already saved anyway,' she says.

Nathan shakes his head and starts the engine.

'I was married once,' he says. 'Yoked to an unbeliever. I prayed for guidance, Laura, prayed like a maniac day and night, especially before uniting in flesh, but the Lord was adamant. She had to go. Like her, you're not spiritually ready.'

The baby scan is on the phone in Laura's pocket, warm against her ass. In the wing mirror, she sees Jared and Falak.

'I'm good, Nathan,' she says.

TERMINAL VELOCITY

T he car judders violently to a halt.

'We ran out of petrol,' says Wil.

A veil of high tensile steel mesh fixed with special bolts and galvanised plates is draped over a steep rocky embankment to their left. What passes as a hard shoulder is a strip of asphalt less than a metre wide, below a fringe of loose rocks. Wil steers into the strip and parks the car.

'Get out. It's not safe,' he says, after a pause.

Normally, Hannah is the more risk-averse one, the more anxious. Even now she finds herself wondering how deep they had to drill the boreholes in the embankment to fix the steel mesh in place. Wil's voice has a quality she doesn't recognise however, a remote quality, as if he's imagining something far worse than she is. Pulling the handle to open the door, a front of freezing cold air blows at once through the car.

'We'll have to stand on the bank. I'll call the AA,' he says.

They wait on the rising bank in the rain, an inch below the wire, in a weird liminal place between road and rock face. Wil tries to get a signal on his phone. It troubles Hannah that she doesn't know the rules about standing there, on the verge, in this no-man's land; it troubles her that she can't read the words on the sign up ahead, although she guesses it's the countdown marker for the exit. Her niece Gwennie plays a game on her iPad called 'Crossy Road'. The aim is to cross an endless series of dual carriageways without dying, timing your character's movements with forensic precision to avoid vehicles, by tapping or swiping on the screen. Hannah imagines stepping into traffic like the character.

'Maybe we should walk towards the exit to get a signal.'

'And leave the car here?' says Wil, baring his teeth.

'It's only a suggestion.'

'No. I'll climb higher,' he says, gesturing towards the embankment. 'If you can get a signal you should phone work.'

'I will in a minute.'

The rain is inside Hannah's clothes and her shoes. It takes all her energy to stop shivering.

'Why can't you just do things straight away?' he says, suddenly. 'Why do you always leave everything until the last minute, make everyone else wait around for you? It's like you think you're above it all, like you don't have to live by the same rules as us mere mortals. If you weren't so late getting up, there'd have been time to get petrol.'

'Where has this come from?' she says. 'Why do you act like you hate me?'

'I don't hate you, I love you,' he says.

They'd met at a rave five years earlier. It was a day of sun and heavy rain, the end of August. The location was a castle on the outskirts of the city, a double-skinned parallelogram with moats and battlements and a leaning tower. He was standing by the doorway to the Great Hall, next to a ceiling corbel, wearing a duffel coat, unaffected by the warm night, the press of bodies. She liked his detachment, his self-composure; the way he'd positioned himself at the edge of things.

Presently she scrambles over the stapled-down rocks towards him. Whenever she remembers that night, she wants to fuck him, reach inside him. But then at other times, she worries she's in the wrong life. With the wrong person. Whereas once she imagined she could be free if she was with him: free and strong, living a life outside of convention, by now his detachment leaves her feeling isolated and needy. She hears him shout a reference number, their car's registration plate.

'I'm on the phone,' he says, putting his hand out to stop her coming closer.

Behind him, an Audi is hurtling towards their car. Bodywork flashing in the rain. Personalised reg plate. The car isn't slowing or moving out or taking any evasive action. Instead it's being driven in a straight line towards them. As if it's on tracks or possessed. As if it's being driven by an algorithm, or by ghosts, or by God.

Hannah can't process what she's seeing. It makes no sense to her. As a child, she always misjudged where the edge of her bed was, misjudged space. She wasn't allowed bunks like her other friends. She had bruises from bumping into the bed post and door frames, so many that the doctor questioned her parents, had her checked for leukaemia. She couldn't dance or catch balls or ride a bike. Whenever she went swimming in the sea, she could never find her way back to the family windbreaker. Now she imagines a rock punching through the steel mesh on the embankment and hurtling down the slope towards Wil. Not to kill him, just get his attention.

'Wil,' she says, 'Please.'

She turns to their parked car on the verge, with its hazards flashing, which is exactly where she thought it would be.

'Stop!' she yells. 'Stop!'

A red hand flaps in front of her like a windsock, bloated from cold and the rain. She recognises it as her hand, her wedding band. The Audi keeps on coming towards them.

When the collision happens, the noise takes so long to reach Hannah's ears it feels like an event in a distant dimension of space: a shredding sound that is more but also less than its parts. Less because there's something slight and eerie about it: distant and unreal and imaginary. More because there are so many things happening at once, the consequences of which Hannah already knows will unravel exponentially into the future, her tiny mind can't contain it.

Hannah remembers an accident her mother had on her way home from church before Christmas. She was pulling the shopping from the boot when she realised that the vehicle, a Land Rover

Discovery, was rolling backwards towards her, crunching over the immaculate pea gravel. Had she forgotten to apply the hand brake? Was she going doolally? She tried jumping in through the driver's side door but lost her footing. One of the new eighteen-inch winter tyres she'd had fitted at the garage a week earlier trundled soundlessly over her wrist.

'I couldn't stop thinking about the meat I'd left in a bag on the ground, a shoulder of lamb,' she said afterwards. 'I didn't feel a thing Hannah.'

After the accident, and the surgery, she bought herself a smaller car, a teal blue Fiesta, on higher purchase, and then enrolled on a course in Archaeology at the University of the Third Age.

'I feel like a new woman,' she kept on saying.

A black disc smashes into the central reservation ahead of them, bouncing off the barrier, yanking Hannah back into the present. Cars spin and swerve around on the carriageway; there is a horrible screeching noise, a slamming down on brakes. A chunk of burgundy metal lands at an angle on the carriageway, across two lanes. The vinyl upholstery on the underside of the metal is so familiar to Hannah it makes her queasy, as does the position of the armrest, the door pocket stuffed with their detritus.

To ease her nausea, to do something, Hannah walks the strip of no-man's land at the bottom of the bank towards the Audi, which has stopped twenty yards ahead of them, the vehicle having spun a hundred and eighty degrees. A man is standing in front of the Audi's hood, oversized grey hands perched on his hips in defiance.

'What the hell was he doing?' he says, pointing at Wil, who is still halfway up the embankment with a queer clenched look on his face. 'He pulled into the lane right in front of me. Didn't indicate.'

'Our car was stationary. We had the hazards on.'

The man sticks his bottom lip out. His suit is coated in what appears to be talcum powder or dandruff.

'I waved. I was on the bank waving. You weren't looking. You were on your phone,' she says.

The moment before the crash is coming back to her. The driver had had his ear to the phone. His lips were flapping, like there was nothing wrong. At his side was a passenger. A woman? The more Hannah stared, the more everything had morphed into a kind of abstract inhuman geometry, a decoupage of flesh-coloured fabrics, the driver's hands on the wheel nothing more than flaccid pink rectangles, the car an arrangement of shapes.

Hannah glances over at Wil again, who hasn't moved yet. In his twenties, before she met him, he hitchhiked across Europe as part of a nine-piece kazoo band playing improvised jazz numbers. Back then he described himself as an existential nihilist who believed that there was no such thing as objective meaning; his friend Midge even shaved a question mark into his buzzcut. Now he was a statistical support officer in the civil service, providing research organisations with access to government data.

'Wil,' she shouts, beckoning.

But it's as though he's still watching the collision, his eyes fixed on the carriageway, as though he's waiting for something else to happen, some kind of denouement, an explanation.

'Came out of nowhere he did,' says the man, his voice faltering. 'Damn air bags went off like a firework. Shit, it's no wonder he's sheepish.'

'Wil,' she yells. 'Over here.'

A woman appears beside the man: older, frailer, trailing the kind of musky, exotic perfume smell Hannah remembers her own mother wearing on family excursions. The woman tugs on the man's sleeve like a child might, loosening the powder from his shoulders. (Powder from the air bag, Hannah realises.)

'I'm Carol, I live in San Diego, by the zoo,' says the woman, who is wearing a red disposable rain poncho, diamante-studded flip flops.

Blood has flooded the white of the woman's right eye. She has a ruby red gash on her brow.

'The orangutan used a crowbar to escape.'

'She's talking about the zoo. San Diego zoo. She has an operation on her mid-brain next week. I was taking her to the airport.'

With a strange asymmetrical grin, Carol waves over at the passing motorists, stopping only when she senses her brother's stern gaze.

'It's like they haven't seen an accident before,' she says.

Wil has appeared at Hannah's side; she wonders how long he's been standing there. His eyes are wide open, as if he's just walked out of the cinema into daylight.

'They could have killed us. We could be dead.'

She nods because what else is there to say.

'I'm going to phone the police,' she says. 'You need to get their details.'

Hannah climbs up the bank to get a better phone signal. A wind has picked up from the west. Everything seems blurry and unreal, but also more real than ever. The man, the Audi, the traffic, the embankment, the mangled remains of their old burgundy hatchback, Wil, her husband of five years, all mediated in maximum resolution, the colours defined, the focus sharp, crystal clear.

If they'd waited in the car, they'd be dead now. Obliterated. Expelled from their vehicle and the universe. Wil was right. He was always right. And yet Hannah has rarely felt calmer or more in control. At the summit of the embankment, with three bars on her phone, she phones the emergency services and then work.

'We broke down on the bypass. A car drove into us.'

'You ok?' says the deputy head Ceri. 'Anybody hurt?'

'Not really, it was a miracle,' she says. We were stationary, they didn't see us.'

'Ffion can take your lessons. Take the day off.'

'I'm okay. I'll be with you by midday.'

Hannah climbs back down the rocks. A few years back, she'd gone on a hen weekend to Morocco. Before going, she saved copies of all her new watercolours to an external hard drive, storing the originals in a locker, along with a note on what to do with them in the event of a plane crash. Wil, who had by then matured from being an existential nihilist to a scientific realist (he preferred the term objectivist), claimed her fear was just narcissism writ large. She had an exaggerated sense of her own importance: the universe didn't revolve around her. It was all to do with the fact that she was an only child, he said, and middle class. 'Middle class as fuck' was his favourite phrase. But then as they were crossing the Channel, there was a sickening sound from the bowels of the plane; everything dropped away from underneath them. Her friend Lena was caught up in trying to stop a nosebleed: blood gushed like hose water from her nostrils. Another friend, the bride-to-be, was crawling down the aisle clutching her smartphone, mewling weirdly like a Siamese cat.

Hannah panicked as much as anybody at first. She couldn't get her head around the idea that although they were still technically alive, they were also already dead. But then suddenly she felt disconnected from all of it: the screaming, the wailing, the grim descent into oblivion. So much of her time was spent ruminating over worst case scenarios: super viruses and meteor strikes, nuclear and climate Armageddon, that when bad things happened, it was as if she was ready for them. Catastrophe was her medium: her element.

Reaching the strip at the foot of the embankment, where Wil and the Audi driver are exchanging insurance details, she walks towards Carol, who is leaning against the passenger side of the Audi, staring at a field of glossy picture book cows beyond the motorway. Carol makes a bizarre thumbs-up sign.

'Hi' she says. 'How the hell are you?'

'Here,' says Hannah, handing her a tissue. 'You have a cut.'

'Don used to work as a driver on film sets,' she says, taking the tissue. 'Did I tell you? He drove de Niro and Scorsese around.'

Carol swipes blood across the rest of her face with the tissue.

'I wanted to get a taxi. He wouldn't listen. He never listens.'

A yellow breakdown service van swerves slowly past the carnage.

'Don't suppose you'll be needing this then!' says the driver, waving a jerry can of petrol through the open window.

'Douchebag,' says Carol, suddenly animated. 'Just fuck off.'

Later, when the police and ambulance arrive, Carol is hurried into the back of the ambulance, surrounded by paramedics. Her brother Don, the Audi driver, is driven to the police station. Zones are demarcated with cones and triangles, barriers are erected, the signs above the motorway switch to gigantic red crosses. A grotesque almost carnival-like atmosphere prevails.

'You've been lucky,' says a police officer, after Wil and Hannah have been checked over by a paramedic and given statements. 'Some people decide to stay in their cars. They think it's safe. Total madness.'

When the police have left, Hannah puts her hand on Wil's knee. Neither of them says anything for a while. After the incident on the aeroplane (clear-air turbulence according to the cabin crew), Hannah had quit her high-paid job as an HR executive at a phone company and retrained as a further ed art teacher. Now she worked part time in a college, painted in her spare time.

'You ok Wil?' she says, finally. 'I called an Uber.'

'That would have been you,' he says, still staring ahead. 'Sitting in the car, waiting to be saved. It's not your fault of course. You're used to everyone doing everything for you. Your parents, yours truly, everybody.'

'I would have got out of the car, Wil. I'm not an idiot.'

'I'm only saying it because I love you,' he says, turning now.

The expensive blue-grey pea coat he bought for the government conference on the future of data in Washington DC is drenched all the way through; his golden wet hair hangs in pieces.

'You're angry and resentful all the time,' she says. 'You're angry with me because you hate your job, because your job isn't who you are, and you resent the fact I quit my job. But it's deeper than that even. You're angry with me because I'm a woman, because I'm allowed to express myself, allowed to be uncertain about things, shit scared even, whereas you feel you have to hold it all in. You're the one who needs saving.'

'If you hate me you should leave me,' he says.

'I didn't say I hated you, for fucks sake.'

Hannah rises to her feet and checks her phone. The Uber is less than a minute away. It pleases her to see it on the map, a little Monopoly car, but real. She knows exactly where it is and why it's coming.

'I need to be back in work by midday,' she says. 'We'll talk later.'

CANNIBAL

.

It tastes delicious: sweet and eggy, like cake mixture straight from the spoon, but with a trace amount of salt that reminds me of something else, something from way back when, before all this.

To suck it up through the cord in one sitting feels wrong: after all, it belongs to both of us, me and her, so I try slowing down, adjusting my flow rate, siphoning off a sneaky millilitre at a time, but for the most part I have zero control. One day, when she catches me hoovering up the entire contents of our replenished food sac, my food cord bulging and throbbing, she pins me with an unblinking stare.

'What happened to you?' she says, after a few seconds have passed. 'You're like that fat sweaty guy on Man Versus Food. It's obscene. Neurotic. There are two of us, in case you hadn't noticed.'

Her eyelids are sewn shut, as are mine, but I know she can see me.

'I'm sorry. I can't help it. I'm famished.'

She tells me again about the other place, the place where she and I were like soul mates. We weren't ourselves, but something else, she says. We were snippets of information, loosely spread across space, a murmuration of birds. We were trying to find something, go somewhere, be something; we didn't know we were happy already.

I look at her askance. Starvation has made her lightheaded.

'There was time before that, too,' she bleats, as I continue gorging. 'When we were in the oceans, in space. Now look at us. Trapped.'

'I don't remember much. You need to eat,' I say.

She bends her head to the side, which is the equivalent of shaking her head.

'It's fast-food,' she says. 'Junk. You need to detox. Clear your head. Then you might remember.'

Unlike the creatures we hear on the outside, neither of us has been reduced to using words yet. Instead, we create ripples in the fluid to communicate, adjusting our position, or trajectory, our movement. The ripples move at different speeds and in different directions.; they vary in size, shape, and depth. We are also, of course, telepathic.

'I've been thinking. Maybe I'm becoming human,' I say, unsure.

Something flickers behind her eyelid as I speak. She pauses, treading water. But then to my astonishment she laughs. She laughs as if I said that I've seen the Virgin Mary in the grooves of our food sac or won the Euro-millions Superdraw twice in a row. The fluid buckles at the outer circumference of her laughter ripples, which signals fear, but also love.

'Human! You're so funny!' she says.

My appetite doubles after that. I am ravenous, insatiable, dog hungry. I could eat eight planets worth of resources. It doesn't help that the food is richer and more complex than before. One day, as I'm gulping down a high-carb appetiser, her food cord gets snagged on my foot.

'It's like Big Foot met the Ugly Sisters,' she says, staring at my foot, whilst going a little blue.

Up until a few sleeps ago, my foot comprised of five ugly protrusions glued together with webbing, just like hers. But now, apart from a strip of flesh that curves downwards like a hangnail from the horror-show that has since become a handsome, thrusting big toe, the webbing has all but vanished. I'm psyched to show off my new appendage, my strength.

'You're just jealous!' I laugh. 'Watch this!'

Bringing a knee toward my chest and extending out my leg,

I fling her off my foot like used toilet tissue, untangling her food cord in the process.

'Whoosh! Back of the net!'

She scuds through the fluid for as long as it takes me to stop whooping with glee, before sinking, unexpectedly, like a shipwreck.

'I thought it would be fun,' I shout down, defensively. 'You should watch where you're going. You're always floating around the place giving people a hard time!'

Later, after an Eat All You Can supper that leaves me more than a little green at the gills, I can't sleep.

I toss and turn.

I have a dream.

In the dream, she and I are hurrying through a pellucid underwater cavern towards a vanishing sliver of daylight. 'This is what we've always dreamed of!' she says. 'It's a one in thirty trillion opportunity.' But as soon as I become aware of the dream, it transforms into something else, something opposite, as if I'm entangled with her on some weird quantum level, and I get the sense that we're being driven forwards not by some creative liberating energy, but by a force that is implacable, despotic, small-minded. 'I want to go back. I've got a bad feeling,' I yell, but she ignores me.

In the morning, as I'm half-way through a bottomless brunch, a fermented broth that leaves a greasy fur on the roof of my mouth, she floats back up from the abyssal zone of the belly bag, sneaking up on me like the Lady in White.

'Christ,' I say. 'I nearly choked then.'

A plume of luminous, silty fluid is leaking from her body like sediment.

'Did you cut yourself?'

She stopped signalling properly yesterday, not long after the drop kick, and I assumed she was giving me the holier-than-thou silent treatment. It wouldn't be the first time. But now that I take a good look at her, I see that her eyes are in the same place as they were weeks ago, pasted to the side of her face like some Victorian circus freak, whereas mine have migrated to the front. She has the same pink nubby hooves as before.

'Look, I know we've had our differences, but I'm worried about you,' I say. 'You should see about your feet, maybe you have bunions? And there's something weird going on with your eyes.'

I don't mention the dream, which I suspect is part memory. I don't mention the fact that without her stupid, starry-eyed idealism, her absurd, misplaced dreams of becoming, we might still be in the other place, free. She retreats into a corner of the belly bag without answering. A hole that I haven't noticed before has opened up in the surface of the bag at her side.

'You should probably move away from the hole.'

For a day and a night afterwards, I can't settle. I lose my appetite. When I'm not forcing myself to eat, I mainline on an anaesthetising torrent of words now streaming through the walls of the belly bag: sleep, eat, wank, shit, drink, like, fuck (my absolute favourite). The delicate, infinitesimal gradations of meaning achieved with ripples or chemical telepathy are such a killjoy in comparison. (Who needs that much info, that much grief?) At the same time, neither food nor light entertainment can distract me from the creeping knowledge that without her there to fill out my dreams, to remind me who we were and what we wanted, this tiny two-bit corner of space and time will be all I know.

I propel myself clumsily towards her, determined to pull her back from the pulsing event horizon of the hole. I'm as fat as a whale, as bloated as a floating corpse, I can barely move. The foot I was so proud of a few weeks ago has mutated into a hook.

'Hang on in there. I'm coming to get you. Don't move.'

The walls of the belly bag rise like a marine trench around her body, and an immense wave of desolation and longing sweeps at once through my body. For a brief moment, I see the cloudy porthole of her eye, the vanishing rusticle of her food cord, then nothing.

When night comes I eat again. I'm a fish bingeing on my own shit. A bottom feeder. I ingest things I shouldn't ingest, things nobody should ingest, things that don't belong to me. I don't ask questions. In the morning, as a strange new undertow yanks me away from the food sac towards the same hole now opening up in the ground, I retch on something sweet and eggy that isn't cake mixture. In it is a sliver of bone.

MONSTROSITY ON STILTS

Lydia is carrying groceries down the driveway to her house when one of the neighbours approaches.

'Jesus Christ. Looks like a bag of bricks,' says Bruce, positioning himself between Lydia and the front door. 'Here, let me help you carry them.'

It's almost the end of January, but Bruce is wearing a bright green Christmas jumper embroidered with the words OH WHAT FUN and faun cargo shorts.

'I'm not quite an invalid yet, Bruce,' says Lydia, stepping sideways to avoid him. 'I'm fine thank you.'

But Bruce won't take no for an answer.

'Pride comes before a fall Lydia,' he says, condescendingly.

Back in the summer, Lydia fell from a stepladder on to the patio while cleaning windows, breaking a finger in the process. The talk in the neighbourhood was that she could no longer look after herself.

'OK then. But could you leave them in the hall—I'm in the middle of sorting?' she says.

It's darker than usual in the hallway: another light bulb has fizzled out. Bruce carries the shopping through the hall and into the kitchen. When he swivels towards Lydia in the doorway to ask her where exactly she wants the bags, a large cyst on his neck radiates a glow-in-the-dark luminosity. Lydia's stomach lurches; a familiar weakness ripples down her legs. It reminds her of being little and lost in the supermarket when you suddenly realise you've been following a stranger down the aisles.

'Anywhere's ok, Bruce,' she says.

In the kitchen, Lydia finds herself offering him a cup of tea.

'White, three sugars, strong,' he says.

Bruce removes a packet of Rich Tea biscuits from a shopping bag. The flesh of his index finger has swollen like bread dough around a signet ring engraved with his family crest. In one showy move, he rips open the biscuit wrapper. His actions send a twinge of dismay through Lydia, who is always careful, reverent, when unwrapping food items.

'Dog biscuits!' he laughs, as she hands him the tea. 'Crime to drink tea dry though.'

'I don't have anything else sorry,' she says.

Bruce talks in detail about his late father Greg, a minor cricket celebrity. Shards of biscuit fly from his mouth as he recounts the time his father drunk beer with Kingsley Amis in a pub near the university. A pellet-sized shard lands on the embroidered 'O' on his jumper. Then, out of nowhere, he asks Lydia if she minds him taking a look at the ongoing building work in her next-door-neighbour's back garden. (The people next door to Lydia, Ceri and Huw, are building a tree house with an internal mezzanine. There are several platforms on different levels, all connected by rope ladders and bridges.)

'Can't see squat from the lodge,' he says.

Bruce lives at the top end of the cul-de-sac in a house named Bay Tree Lodge, which has a porch with Doric columns, fancy wraparound railings, and synthetic bright green turf that needs vacuuming.

'Oh ok,' she says. 'But you'll have to come upstairs.'

Lydia leads Bruce to the only bedroom that directly overlooks the next-door-neighbour's garden: her bedroom. He follows far too close to her body, his breath damp and biscuity on the part of her scalp where the hair has thinned out. He is bigger than her late husband Gordon, at least six foot tall, with thick wrists and big feet, and she can sense him looming over her like weather.

'How's Margaret?' she says, to break the silence.

Margaret is Bruce's wife. When Gordon died a year ago, Margaret brought Lydia a casserole of chicken supreme, two packets of Uncle Ben's boil-in-the-bag rice, and a mini bottle of

Pinot Grigio. Although the Pinot Grigio was still in the pantry, Lydia was inordinately grateful for Margaret's kindness.

Bruce pauses on the stair tread behind Lydia.

'Who? The Ice Maiden?!' he says, laughing darkly.

Rumour has it that Margaret has since moved into a pavilion garden room in the grounds of the lodge with her old Siberian forest cat, Ziggy, and has cashed in a couple of savings bonds to splash out on Botox, fillers, and cheek augmentation. Lydia would normally disapprove of such actions, but in Margaret's case she's strangely gratified.

'I didn't mean to pry, Bruce,' she says.

Within seconds they have reached the back bedroom.

'Christ. It's a whopper,' says Bruce, peering out. 'Forty grand's worth. Minimum. You can only see half of it from the lodge.'

Lydia joins him by the window overlooking Huw and Ceri's garden, standing to the side to make room.

'He'll need retrospective planning permission. Section 36. Town and Country Planning Act. For anything over thirty centimetres above ground level.'

The treehouse is at least two and half metres above ground: a large hexagonal structure that girdles an ash tree in the middle of Huw and Ceri's garden. It isn't the size of the treehouse that troubles Lydia so much as the random shapes and the mix of materials: the spiralling decks, swirling around the treehouse walls, the safety netting around the hammock bridge that looks like hair, the shingle cladding like scales, the way the whole thing sprawls into every corner of the garden. Every aspect of it makes Lydia think of some giant sleeping vertebrate.

'They'll be able to see into your bedroom,' says Bruce, turning.

In the last few days, a new platform, supported by diagonal braces, has sprung up around a smaller tree next to Lydia's boundary fence. If Gordon was alive, he'd have gone straight over there, given them what for.

'I know that, Bruce,' she says.

Bruce stinks of cats, Lydia realises. Beneath the stench of felines is another smell: a tanginess that she associates with uncleanliness. This new detail confuses Lydia greatly, as Bruce is a successful professional with his own five-star dental practice specialising in veneers. The dental practice is spotlessly clean.

'Lucky bastards!' he says.

On the washing line below the window, an old, discoloured flannel flaps in a gust of westerly wind. Something curious settles on Lydia's right buttock. It takes her several seconds to realise that the *something* is her neighbour's hand.

'Bruce,' she says.

Bruce removes his hand almost instantly, but not before Lydia has assimilated the slow spread of his fingers across her buttocks, the dull uneven series of vibrations as he transfers weight from one finger to the next, like those weird, water-walking bugs.

'Monstrosity on stilts,' he says loudly, as if nothing happened. 'Outrageous.'

Lydia edges further away from her neighbour, now noticing how the bottom left-hand corner of the window is fogged up around the seals.

'Though, coming to think of it, you could take out half the bloody village from up there. Pick them off one by one. First-class hide for a sniper.'

Bruce laughs at his own joke, a laugh that sounds like a single, stretched-out suck.

'Well, must put the ice cream away,' says Lydia.

As they descend the stairs to return to the kitchen, Bruce maintains his distance, but Lydia can still feel the imprint of his hand on her buttock. It wasn't only the groping that had unsettled her, it was also the idea that he'd done it to poke fun at her, to draw attention to the sag of her bum. She was at least ten years his senior.

'You shouldn't take it lying down, Lydia' he says. 'You should write to the council.'

Lydia's foot hovers in the air above the tread, as if her brain has miscalculated the height of the stair risers. The handrail feels lower, the staircase run steeper, and yet she has lived in this house for close to three decades now; she remembers Rhys and Betsan sliding down the handrail, shrieking with glee. 'Mammy!

Mammy! Come and see!' Lowering her foot on to the tread, Lydia grips the handrail even tighter.

'I couldn't even get planning for my balcony decking,' says Bruce. 'Bloody travesty.'

Lydia can't believe he's still talking. Perhaps he thinks that by yapping on loudly about planning and treehouses and balconies, she will forget what just happened. With an odd sense of climbing up to reach land, even though in reality she's going downstairs, Lydia reaches the bottom tread of the staircase. As she does so the phone springs into life.

The caller is her distant cousin David, who is the only person besides Rhys and Betsan who phones Lydia on the landline. David lives in an old rundown static in Trecco Bay caravan park and was recently selected for deep brain stimulation to treat unexplained hand tremors. In his spare time, he creates hand-drawn subway maps for fictional places, including connecting bus routes, ferry routes, and transit hubs. It remains a mystery to Lydia how he can still draw the maps.

'You can go now, Bruce,' says Lydia, holding the handset. 'I need to take this. It's my cousin.'

'What about the ice cream?' asks the neighbour. 'You needed to put the ice cream away?'

'Ice cream? Oh, I meant peas. Don't know if I'm coming or going!' says Lydia, covering the mouthpiece.

Lydia hasn't bought any ice cream. It was a white lie to get Bruce out of the bedroom. Even the tiniest spoonful of ice cream sends skewers of icy pain from the top of Lydia's skull to halfway down her spine.

'How about I put the peas away then? I'm here to help, Lydia.'

'No! It's ok!' says Lydia. 'But thank you Bruce, for your help, with the bags.'

Bruce remains rooted to the spot, glassy-eyed and gleaming by the sidelight. The crumb of biscuit is no longer stuck to the embroidered 'O' on his jumper. Suddenly he becomes agitated. Stuffs his hand in to his pocket. Pulls out keys. Lydia registers a mini Tesco Clubcard, a supermarket trolley fob, a pink pig pompom she imagines belongs to Margaret. He uses the tip of a key to scratch his femur.

'So, what's your favourite flavour then?' he asks, stepping closer.

Lydia has no idea what he's talking about. Do peas come in different flavours?

'Mine is rum n raisin,' he says, stretching his neck out like a bird from within the collared folds of his Christmas jumper and then thrusting his chin out. 'Bet you're more *vanilla?*'

Lydia has a sudden vision of the neighbour probing her brain with his fingers, parting the fleshy clefts between her neurones. He steps closer and she pushes him away. At first he seems not to react. A strange, lopsided smirk tears slowly from left to right across his face. Then, in cartoonish slow motion, he topples backwards to the ground, flailing as if the carpet is ice.

'Oh my god. Sorry,' she says. 'Not sure what happened. I didn't mean to—'

Bruce is lying flat on his back, like a housefly. He levers himself clumsily into sitting position. As Lydia helps him back to his feet, she hears David speaking on the other side of the line, describing the neuropsychiatric side effects of his surgery. Before the surgery, he'd hallucinated a whole new public transport system for an imaginary island called Tameran, a supercontinent called Antumnos, and a bewildering futuristic city called Golud. But since the surgery, he's had difficulty concentrating.

'Do you need an ambulance?' she says to Bruce. 'I'll phone for an ambulance.'

'Fucking whackjobs, the lot of you,' says Bruce.

After he's gone, Lydia rests on the seat that's attached to the telephone table until the light drains from the side window by the door, going over the afternoon's events in her head. Although she can't remember the exact moment she shoved Bruce to the floor, she assumes it must have been some kind of primal defence mechanism, a reflex. In her imagination, Bruce is not even the neighbour anymore, but a shadowy scavenger, lying in wait. And yet, she shouldn't have pushed him.

When it's too cold to stay in the hallway any longer, Lydia

finishes putting the shopping away in the kitchen and seals the ruptured biscuit wrapper with a clip. Sensing the stray biscuit pellet somewhere on the carpet, sticky with Bruce's spit, she also hurriedly vacuums the hallway.

When she returns upstairs to her bedroom for a lie-down, these days she takes naps in the late afternoon, naps that bleed into one another like day into dusk, the treehouse is still there, waiting for her, the new platform reaching out like a timber tongue, the bridge shivering in the early evening breeze. Lydia rushes over to the bed. Falling into a fitful sleep, she wakes to a monochromatic streak of morning twilight filtering through the curtains.

Next door's garden is illuminated by a series of LED security lights she hasn't noticed before, and Lydia soon realises that it's not twilight but night. One of the security lights is attached to the shingle cladding on the treehouse; another to a post at the rear of the garden; another to safety rails surrounding the platform overlooking her bedroom.

Using Gordon's old binoculars, Lydia leans out of the window to get a closer look. The edge of the platform is cantilevering over her property line, half a metre beyond the boundary fence. If she were younger, she could have leaped on to the platform from her windowsill and camped there like a fugitive. But her brief excitement at the idea of stealing away in secret, hiding in time, turns into a disorienting vertigo that makes her queasy. The treehouse is growing more reptilian by the day; everything is closing in on her. Gripping the windowsill, Lydia feels her legs go; she can't move. It was bad enough that Huw and Ceri hadn't consulted her about their plans, that to them she was just the old lady from the corner house, an irrelevance, but the fact they'd now begun to appropriate her garden with their treehouse, as if she was already dead, well, it was too much, too much.

Finally, she makes it downstairs. It was time for a cup of tea. Tea settled her. Over the last few days, as construction of the new platform in Huw and Ceri's garden had gathered pace, Lydia had even considered moving to Anglesey to be with Betsan. But now the idea made her blood boil. Why should she move? The house belonged to Gordon and her. Hell, the house *still* belonged to her. And as for Bruce and his funny business, well, she was almost sure that he wouldn't return. And yet, there was more than one way to dispossess a person, for one thing you could fail to take them seriously, and Lydia knew that unless she took control of the situation, her psychic survival was at stake. But what could she do?

Carrying the cup of tea back upstairs, Lydia pauses in front of the door to the integral garage. Back when Gordon was alive, she'd often retreat to the garage for peace and quiet, take a Thermos flask, the latest crime thriller. It was a good place to rest and recharge, to think and weigh up options, to get a different perspective on things. The garage was in effect a kind of no-man's land, where everything was in limbo, either on its way out of the house, or on its way back in, its value still up for negotiation. It was a space where the meaning and purpose of everything could be reimagined or reinvented. And although Lydia hasn't set foot in the garage since Gordon died, she is suddenly compelled to go inside.

The garage is even colder than she remembers. Reaching for the light switch inside the door, the drop in temperature is so dramatic it's as if she's stepped off a plane into a foreign country. Lydia's mind returns to her cousin David's fictional landscapes. Weirdly, she always recognised the places he described, even though they didn't exist. *I've been to that city*, she'd think. *I've seen that port*. It was maybe this that connected them: this shared belief in somewhere else, some place where they could finally be themselves.

Lydia walks further out into the hinterland of the garage, still uncertain of her mission. A petrol chainsaw languishing on a metal shelving rack draws her attention. Running her fingers along the cold alloy guide bar, she imagines sawing off the treehouse legs, slicing through the rope bridge, amputating the appendage that encroached into her garden. That would show them! But no, that wasn't her style. It was too unseemly. Too uncouth. Flicking on another light on the far wall, a rosewood tallboy belonging to her grandmother rears majestically into view. Lydia pulls out one empty drawer after another, looking for inspiration, redemption, but it isn't until she opens the secret drawer carved into the moulded top lip of the tallboy that she finds it.

Dawn is slowly sweeping upwards over the treeline as Lydia hurries down the path towards next door's back garden, her gardening clogs slapping the slabs, a green spray tank attached like a military assault pack to her back. Huw and Ceri are away on another mini break; no need to be careful.

Stepping into the beam of a security light, Lydia places the old ice cream tub of tools she found in the tallboy on a gravelled area around the tree closest to her boundary fence. Dropping the spray tank to the ground, she empties the tub of its contents: rubberized work gloves, a canister of Roundup, Gordon's face respirator.

When she has finished filling the spray tank with the Roundup solution and then repressurized the tank with the plunger lid, Lydia pulls on Gordon's respirator mask. Normally she doesn't like things on her face, the filter boxes on either side of the mask are heavier than they appear, but the cold morning air filtering through the valves sharpens her resolve, and she finds the task of adjusting the head straps manageable, almost satisfying.

Picking up the spray tank in Gordon's gloves, Lydia follows the perimeter of an imaginary circle around the tree that supports the newest platform, and then begins to slowly spray the trunk with the fluid. It's like a ceremonial dance, she thinks. One of those maypole dances that ushers in Spring.

As she follows the circle to the other side of the tree, a blue glow from an upstairs bedroom in Bay Tree Lodge suggests Bruce could be watching through the window. Lydia continues spraying regardless, unperturbed, thrilled even, adjusting the settings on the spray nozzle so that the flow rate and pressure are increased. A bright, thin, cherry-coloured fluid hits the bark like a series of arrows, seeping like blood into the small corner of land that she's reclaiming.

SiAN HuGHES

Sian Hughes is a copywriter, creative practitioner, screenwriter, and writer whose stories have appeared in print and in online magazines, including 'Scribble', 'The Fiction Pool' and 'Storgy'. 'Death and the Teenage Stripper' was a runner-up in The Rhys Davies International Short Story Competition. 'Shaving for Dog' was shortlisted for the Fish Short Story Prize.

A few of Sian's stories have also been adapted into short films. An adaptation of 'Consumed' was premiered at the Glasgow Short Film Festival 2021, whilst 'Marw Stripio', a Welsh language adaptation of 'Death and the Teenage Stripper', was screened on BBC Wales as part of the 'Saith Ffilm Fer' season.

Screenwriting credentials include 'Natural Cures for Common Ailments', broadcast on HTV Wales, as well as scripts co-written with young people as part of the Arts Council of Wales's 'Lead Creative Schools Scheme', including 'Wenglish', which won first prize in the Media 4 Schools Animation Awards.

Sian recently completed an MA in Creative Writing at the Open University and is working on a novel provisionally entitled 'Dead in a Good Way', based on her story of the same name. 'Pain Sluts' was written with financial support from a Literature Wales 'Writers Bursary'.

Visit Sian's official website: https://sianhughes.me.uk
Follow Sian on Twitter: @FlossingtheCat

Authior photo by Claire Cousin

ACKNOWLEDGEMENTS

There are so many people to thank - and so little space to do it in.

So, in no particular order, thank you to my family, who are of course my entire world. My husband Philip John, who never stopped believing in me, and my children Lili, Aaron, and Nel, the loveliest and most miraculous creatures on Earth. I love you.

Thank you to my extended family, who were there in the beginning. My guardian angel from way back when, Mamgu Treforus, my mother Elisabeth, my father Gerald, no longer with us physically but present in every other way, and my brother Dewi. (Not forgetting Meinir, and my nieces and nephew Dafydd, Mari, and Leisa, whose love of reading takes me back to my childhood.)

Thanks to my awesome tribe of friends, who kept me sane, and fed me treats. Helen, Lowri, Liz H, Jane, Liz R, Rachel, Claire, Megan, Emily, Emma, Charlotte, Alison, and the firebrands otherwise known as The Llandeilo Girls. You know who you are - and what you've done!

A final colossal thank you to my writing mentors, the late great English teacher Anne Walters, Jules Horne, my inspirational creative writing tutor at the Open University, and the team at STORGY Books, Tomek, Anthony, and Ross, but most of all to Tomek, who fuelled only by Aperol and a passion for independent publishing, painstakingly worked on every incarnation of every story, and whose words of encouragement gave me the confidence to keep on writing.

Diolch yn fawr, you're all lush.

COMING SOON FROM STORGY BOOKS

FLAMINGO MIST

TOMAS MARCANTONIO

"A beautiful mash-up of grim noir and Japanese flare with a beating heart of motorhead vigilantes. Sons of Anarchy meets Sin City."
– Dan Stubbings –
The Dimension Between Worlds

SONAYA NIGHTS - BOOK TWO

Sonaya, 2052. Estranged from old allies and stalked by a crooked government, one-eared ex-con Daganae Kawasaki remains shrouded by shadows, deserted and desperate to locate his estranged young daughter. But as the body count rises and drones scour the streets, Dag is forced into the most sordid corners of Sonaya in his hunt for answers. As the neon nerves of home blaze bright, a labyrinth of alleys hides a colourful cast, each engaged in a different and more dangerous game as an unwitting Dag soon discovers himself as the missing piece.

To discover more about FLAMINGO MIST visit
STORGY.COM

ALSO AVAILABLE FROM STORGY BOOK

THE
DARK STATE TRILOGY
BOOK ONE

Featuring the finalists of STORGY Magazines's Annihilation Radiation Short Story Competition the Annihilation Radiation Anthology contains 18 short stories by an array of talented apocalyptic authors. The Annihilation Radiation Anthology explores three era's of atomic annihilation; Before, During, and After. So zip up your hazmat suit and hunker in your bunker with Book One of STORGY'S Dark State Trilogy.

ANNIHILATION
RADIATION

To discover more about ANNIHILATION RADIATION visit STORGY.COM

ALSO AVAILABLE FROM STORGY BOOK

YOU ARE NOT ALONE

HELPING PEOPLE AFFECTED BY HOMELESSNESS

With great thanks to contributing authors, artists, and designers, STORGY Books is proud to present You Are Not Alone; An Anthology of Hope and Isolation. Working in close partnership with UK charities The Big Issue Foundation (registered charity number 1049077), Centrepoint (292411), Shelter (263710), and The Bristol Methodist Centre (1150295), You Are Not Alone will help raise funds and provide support for people affected by homelessness following the devastating outbreak of Coronavirus. For far too long the most vulnerable within our communities have suffered in isolation, abandoned and ignored, voiceless. But we hear our hurting kin; and this is our reply.

You Are Not Alone is an exclusive anthology of short stories and poems featuring a carefully curated cast of international award-winning and emerging authors, including Susmita Bhattacharya, Astra Bloom, Kathy Fish, Tim Lebbon, Toby Litt, Adam Lock, Carmen Marcus, Benjamin Myers, Rahul Raina, Adrian J Walker, and many many more.

To discover more about YOU ARE NOT ALONE visit
STORGY.COM

ALSO AVAILABLE FROM STORGY BOOKS

SHALLOW CReek

This is the tale of a town on the fringes of fear, of ordinary people and everyday objects transformed by terror and madness, a microcosm of the world where nothing is ever quite what it seems. This is a world where the unreal is real, where the familiar and friendly lure and deceive. On the outskirts of civilisation sits this solitary town. Home to the unhinged. Oblivion to outsiders.

Shallow Creek contains twenty-one original horror stories by a chilling cast of contemporary writers, including stories by Sarah Lotz, Richard Thomas, Adrian J Walker, and Aliya Whitely. Told through a series of interconnected narratives, Shallow Creek is an epic anthology that exposes the raw human emotion and heart-pounding thrills at the genre's core.

To discover more about SHALLOW CREEK visit STORGY.COM

ALSO AVAILABLE FROM STORGY BOOKS

...EXIT EARTH...

EXIT EARTH delves into dystopian worlds and uncovers the most daring and original voices in print today. With twenty-four short stories, accompanying artwork, afterwords, and interviews, EXIT EARTH is a haunting exploration of the sanity of our species...past, present, and future.

Featuring the fourteen finalists from the STORGY EXIT EARTH Short Story Competition, and additional stories by award winning authors M.R. Carey (The Girl with all the Gifts), Toby Litt (Corpsing, DeadKidSongs), Courttia Newland (The Gospel According to Cane, A Book of Blues), James Miller (Sunshine State, Lost Boys), and David James Poissant (The Heaven of Animals). With accompanying artwork by Amie Dearlove, HarlotVonCharlotte, and CrapPanther.

To discover more about EXIT EARTH visit
STORGY.COM

We hope you enjoyed Pain Sluts and your literary excusrion into STORGY Books.

On behalf of everyone at STORGY - and all our authors - we would like to thank you for your invaluable support of independent publishing.

We will forever cherish your belief and backing of the books we publish.

Thank You!

ONLINE ARTS & ENTERTAINMENT MAGAZINE

BOOKS - FILMS - ART - MUSIC
INTERVIEWS - REVIEWS - SHORT STORIES

For more information about STORGY Magazine visit our
website.

STORGY

www.storgy.com

 @fb.me/morest0rgy @morestorgy morestorgy

Lightning Source UK Ltd.
Milton Keynes UK
UKHW011433260422
402070UK00001B/26

9 781916 325845